W9-AQR-385

A HOLLYWOOD TALE
OF LOVE AND MURDER

A HOLLYWOOD TALE
OF LOVE AND MURDER

A NOVEL

BY

DIANE BRENDA BRYAN

Copyright © 2010 by Diane Brenda Bryan.

ISBN: Hardcover   978-1-4415-9117-3
               Softcover   978-1-4415-9116-6

All rights reserved. No part of this book may be reproduced or transmitted in any form
or by any means, electronic or mechanical, including photocopying, recording, or by
any information storage and retrieval system, without permission in writing from the
copyright owner.

This is a work of fiction. Names, characters, places and incidents either are the product
of the author's imagination or are used fictitiously, and any resemblance to any actual
persons, living or dead, events, or locales is entirely coincidental.

This book was printed in the United States of America.

To order additional copies of this book, contact:
Xlibris Corporation
1-888-795-4274
www.Xlibris.com
Orders@Xlibris.com
70584

DEDICATION

To all who would be, and are, thespians
In that glorious make-believe land of
HOLLYWOOD

WITH LOVE

To my children: Jonathan, E'lyn and Jeffrey
To my extended family, Kim and John and the grandkids

WITH THANKS

To my colleagues: David Shapiro (in memorium),
Donald Silverman, and Dr. Kurt F. Stone
For their words of wisdom

SPECIAL KUDOS

To E'lyn Bryan, for her "tech" support

"The web of our life is of a mingled yarn,
Good and ill together."
William Shakespeare

CHAPTER ONE

MEXICO 1999

The old woman pulled her shawl tightly around her shivering body. The wind was picking up and soon it would be dusk and grow dark. She hastened her pace as she trudged along the dusty road that would pass the cemetery of the *Noche de Muertos* on her way to the town dump, on the outskirts of Tzurumutaro. Her old dog Amigo walked wearily along by her side. This weekly adventure was becoming more difficult for Carmelita and her aging companion. She was ever mumbling to herself, "You are too old and too weak, *Vieja*, but who is there in this sorry place to help an ancient one such as you?" She bent to pat her companion on the head.

Tonight was no different except that she had left her dismal abode later than usual. She gripped her walking stick tightly. "Old faithful friend, we have work to do. We must find something worthwhile to sell for a few *pesos*." Amigo wagged his tail in agreement.

Almost out of breath, she finally arrived at her destination. Grey streamers of dusk with interceding ribbons of orange were already swirling about the sky. Yes, it will be dark soon. I must hurry. She poked about the trash around her and groused about her circumstances, as usual, sotto voce. The sky darkened; she quickened her pace. Suddenly, her walking stick stalled against something it couldn't budge. Amigo whined loudly, sniffing, paws scratching the ground. The deepening shadows made it almost impossible for Carmelita's tired eyes to discern what lay there. "What have you found, my trusty one? Something you are not strong enough to move, eh?"

She bent down, squinting and jutting her face closer to the ground. Looks like something wrapped up. Maybe something I can sell. She extended her right hand and instantly recoiled in horror. Whatever it was, it crumbled at her touch like flakes of burnt paper. "Aiey! What is this?" She reached out again and when her hand touched the charred remains of a human foot emerging from a burnt plastic bag, she became hysterical. "*Asesinato! Asesinato!* Help! Help!"

The pudgy watchman at the far end of the dump was dozing. The woman's screams jolted him out of his reverie. What is happening? This has always been such a quiet, boring job; now someone is shouting "Murder". For assurance, he wrapped his fingers around the small gun in his jacket as he turned on the huge flashlight that hung from his belt. Walking in the direction of Carmelita's voice, he yelled, "Who's there? What's wrong? Where are you?"

"Here, here," the hysterical woman answered. "I am over here, hurry."

He followed the sound of her voice and soon found the old woman. She stood quaking and sobbing, pointing at the dark mass on the ground.

"What is it? What are you pointing at, old woman?" He followed her shaking finger pointing to a place on the ground. As he knelt, his flashlight revealed partially burnt plastic garbage bags in which were dismembered body parts.

An immediate call to the police brought a response within a short time. Soon, headlights illuminated the area. The officer in charge questioned the old lady and the watchman and then conducted a preliminary examination of the scene. The Chief of Police tipped his hat back on his head, rubbed the side of his face and chin, and just stared. It was not unusual for body parts to turn up in places such as these, but nothing of this sort had happened here before. "Rope off this area. Nobody touch anything."

He then placed a call to the Coroner's Office in Mexico City for an ambulance. "Let us see what we can make of this poor soul's remains."

CHAPTER TWO

CALIFORNIA 1996

Charles Markham, Christine O'Hara and Blake Dugan all arrived in Hollywoodland in the 1990's. Each didn't know the other existed. The only thing they had in common was the ambition to 'make it big' in the movie business. They could not have anticipated how their lives would intertwine.

*   *   *

Charles Markham was a handsome 6'2", lean and muscular, with steel blue eyes and refined features, framed by a good head of black hair. At Ohio U., he had developed an intense interest in photography which, eventually, instilled in him the desire to become a motion picture cameraman. He worked with local picture production companies, honing his craft. When he announced his desire to go to Hollywood, his parents agreed to finance his dream until he found employment.

Not long after his arrival in Los Angeles, he took up residence in a small hotel where he became friendly with many of the guests, who were mainly actors. They would gather together evenings in one of the local eateries to exchange information about their daily travels to casting offices. Charles got some good leads from them about available jobs on camera crews. He was well liked because of his fine character and his willingness to be of help whenever necessary. And, he had a down to earth nature and honesty . . . a bit rare in movieland.

One evening, a newcomer joined the group. Margot Mercer was a pretty ingénue type, full of hope and ambition. She and Charles were immediately smitten with each other. They soon began dating exclusively. When an apartment became available on Hollywood Boulevard, Charles decided to rent it. Staying at the hotel had become financially prohibitive.

He and Margot dated for several months. Charles was employed; she was making rounds. When she began hinting that her funds were running out and she would have to make a decision about returning home to Wisconsin, Charles suggested she move in with him. After all, their relationship had morphed into a serious one. Why not?

Her response caught him by surprise.

"Charles, this may be Hollywood where nothing is real, but if our feelings for each other **are** real, I want us to be married."

This was a development for which he had not been prepared, but the fear of losing her was primary. He bent on one knee, placed his right hand above his heart, and asked, "Will you marry me, Margot?"

*   *   *

Charles had a good job as "Best Boy" on a film already in progress. He lucked out when one of the cameramen took ill. Learning the ropes quickly, he soon earned a good reputation for creativity and innovation. as a cameraman. After a grueling day behind the camera, he looked forward to coming home, a relaxing dinner with Margot and listening to her energized accounts of job hunting.

Before long, the stories decreased and excuses for not making the rounds increased. Charles tried to encourage her. "Sweetheart, don't be discouraged. It's tough but sooner or later, you'll make it. Just hang in there."

One evening, she exploded. "I'm sick and tired of the rat race. I would love to stay home and take care of you . . . and let you take care of me."

First love does not know how to refuse.

Before long, it became evident that Margot had other ideas. The bills from her shopping sprees began piling up. Nightly, Charles came home to an apartment in disarray—no dinner waiting—no Margot. Her excuse, when she finally showed up, was either she had been out with friends or shopping late. "I'm sorry. I didn't have time to prepare anything. Let's eat out."

Eating out became routine . . . even the sex. And, nothing could salvage what had become unbearable for Charles. Love turned into anger, resentment and disillusionment.

Their parting was not pleasant.

*   *   *

Los Angeles has always been the land of sunshine and fun for most of its inhabitants. Not so for Charles Markham. After his devastating divorce, he opted more and more to spend his time alone. He found no redeeming features in the City of Angels—only in his work.

He now enjoyed a high salaried job as a cinematographer, yet he opted to live in a small apartment off Sunset Boulevard where he led a frugal existence, monetarily and emotionally. The apartment was sparsely furnished in typical single-man fashion and his bedroom closet was inhabited by prêt-a-porter suits and shirts, with economically priced accessories. He took heart in the fact that soon he would be finished paying off the divorce debts. Maybe his life would change for the better without the Sword of Damocles hanging over his head. Meanwhile, he shied away from neighbors.

There was one close friend, Jim Green, who joined him at times for a couple of beers and conversation, usually in Charles' apartment. In spite of Charles' idiosyncrasies, Jim liked him and figured he'd gradually come around and become more outgoing. He constantly joked with him. "When are you going to start living a little?" Jim didn't push too hard because he believed Charles needed more time to get over his failed marriage.

Charles would smile weakly, in response. "One of these days. Not just yet."

*   *   *

One evening at the Irish Pub, a neighborhood watering hole, Charles was unusually talkative. "You know, I gave that bitch everything she wanted, but she just nagged and complained all the time. Ran me ragged . . ."

"Yeah, I know how some women can be," Jim agreed. "That's why I'm still a bachelor and take my fun whenever and wherever."

"Don't you ever get lonely? Sometimes I think I can't handle it."

Jim looked at his friend, amazed. This was the first time he opened up about anything personal. "Well, old Buddy, you gotta do like I do. Stop ignoring the femmes fatales. Have a good time once in a while."

The Irish Pub was a hangout for newspapermen like Jim and movie people. That night Jim sat facing the length of the bar and couldn't help noticing the woman who sat alone at the other end. She was attractive in the way of most women indigenous to the Hollywood scene. Long auburn tresses framed a beautifully chiseled face. From what he could tell, she was built well.

Christine O'Hara couldn't help but notice the two good-looking men deep in conversation at the opposite end of the bar. She sipped her drink and watched, trying to figure out what was transpiring. One of them looked down in the dumps; the other seemed to be trying to cheer him up. She thought about asking Tim, the bartender, if he knew them but decided to encourage their attention in her own way.

She stood up suddenly and walked slowly in their direction. If necessary, the ladies' room was just past them on the left. Charles sat with his back to her, but Jim became aware of the statuesque beauty approaching them. "Hey, heads up, Charlie-boy. Gorgeous chick heading our way. I'll show you how it's done."

"Okay. Sure." Charles took another gulp of his drink.

"Hi Darlin'. Lookin' good. Care to have a drink with a couple of lonesome bachelors?" Jim stood up.

Christine returned a radiant smile. "Would love to . . . if you promise to behave," she teased, perching on the barstool Jim offered. She extended her hand. "I'm Christine O'Hara."

"I'm Jim Green and this is my best friend, Charles Markham. He needs a little cheering up. Think you can help out?"

She answered with a smile more radiant than before. "I will certainly try." Christine couldn't help but notice the way Charles' eyes narrowed. This will be difficult.

Jim's thoughts were introspective but along different lines. Great looking broad. If old Buddy-boy here's not interested, I sure as hell am.

The next couple of hours were spent in drinking and lively chatter. Charles warmed up and began enjoying himself, much to his surprise. Jim's right. Gotta loosen up.

The bartender was accustomed to Christine's friendly nature. It was good for his business but he kept a watchful eye on her. On occasion, he would buy her a drink on the house before closing. Somehow, he sensed tonight would be different.

When he announced, "Last call", Jim ordered another round and "one more to back us up". He wanted to keep the party going. Charlie-boy was really showing promise. They finished their drinks and, with arms around each other, exited singing, "The party's over. It's time to call it a day . . ."

"Are we calling it a day? There's lots of night left," Jim encouraged.

Christine commented, "Nothing's open this late."

"Well, how about my place?" Charles suggested, surprising himself.

A flabbergasted Jim said, "Well, okay then. Your place it is. You in, Christine?"

"You betcha!"

*   *   *

It took only one more beer for Jim to pass out on the couch. It wasn't the first time. Charles was pretty much out of it, too, but not so much that he couldn't respond to temptation. The music coming from the radio was soft and romantic.

"Come on, Charles, let's dance. This music is great." Christine extended her arms.

"I'm not much of a dancer."

"Oh, I'll bet you're terrific." She took his hand and led him to the small, open area in the living room. As she turned to him, swaying, moving closer, he compulsively locked her in his arms, kissing her hungrily on her willing lips. She returned his passion. She was accustomed to bar flirtations but rarely ended up in a guy's apartment. Tonight, somehow, was different. She couldn't explain it, but this Charles touched a nerve. He intrigued her: Attractive, aloof—but vulnerable. Definitely a challenge.

Suddenly, Charles released her and turned away. "I'm sorry. I shouldn't have kissed you like that. Maybe you should go. You've aroused feelings in me I've avoided for a long time."

This was a first for Christine. Usually, she was the one that had to cajole her way out. She touched his arm lightly. "Please, Charles, it's all right. I'm feeling the same way." She stopped. Not going to argue the point. That could be a complete turn-off. If she wanted to see him again, she sensed she had to play the game his way. She longed to kiss him again but, instead, she dropped her hand to her side. "It's all right."

"Sorry, Christine. I don't want to take advantage of you. We've had a lot to drink. Let me take you home."

She responded, almost in a whisper, "If that's what you want . . ." She picked up her purse and walked to the door.

On the couch, Jim snorted loudly, mumbled contentedly and rolled over.

The walk in the fresh, early morning air had a sobering affect. Christine spoke about growing up on a small farm in Kansas and how she looked forward to going to the town movie house once a month. "I became so enthralled with the beautiful, talented people on the screen, I wanted to be one of them. My drama coach in high school convinced my parents to allow me to pursue an acting career. He was impressed by my willingness to undertake the most difficult of roles . . . and I did receive a few awards . . ."

"Which I'm sure you deserved." Charles liked her enthusiasm, among other things. If this 5'8" beauty had the talent to match, she was a sure winner. Couldn't be more than twenty-three years old . . . wonder if I could help her?

His reverie was interrupted. "Here we are."

She lived in one of the apartment complexes on North Sycamore, off Hollywood Boulevard. At the entrance, Charles bent forward to kiss Christine lightly on the cheek. "I'll see you up to your apartment."

In the elevator, she pushed the button for the 10th floor. At her door, Charles said, "I'd like to see you again," surprising himself once more.

"Ditto, Baby." With that, she suddenly pulled him to her and kissed him hard on the lips.

Flustered, he said a shaky "Goodnight. I'll call you," and turned abruptly toward the elevator.

She yelled after him, "I'm in the phone book." As she closed the door behind her, she smiled. Maybe not so difficult after all.

Charles hurried his steps. Gotta unload this on Jimbo.

The apartment was empty.

*   *   *

When Charles and Jim got together later in the week, Charles was animated as he recalled the events of that evening with Christine. Jim could tell she had made quite an impression and was happy that his friend was thinking of seeing her again. After a few beers, he suggested, "Let's go to the Pub. Maybe your girlfriend will show," he teased.

This irritated Charles. "I don't want to just run into her . . . told her I'd phone. Stop calling her my girlfriend. I hardly know her."

"What's there to know? That kiss you described was pretty serious stuff, if you ask me."

"Well, I'm not asking you. I'll handle this my way."

"Flaming idiot," Jim muttered, reaching for another beer.

At this stage of his life, Charles was neither inclined to be impetuous nor adventurous in the romance arena. Since that evening with Christine, he spent a lot of time mulling things over. The little voice that challenged him on occasion was now nagging at him.

Go for it, man. It's been a long time. But the other voice—the cautious one—kept interfering. Be careful, Buster. The last time you got carried away, you paid a huge price.

Yet, he couldn't erase the sensation, the arousal in him, when Christine's voluptuous breasts pressed against him as she drew him tightly to her; nor could be forget the sweep of her tongue as she kissed him. Sometimes, self-discipline can be a pain in the butt. He hadn't felt so stimulated in a long time, but he couldn't pursue what was obviously mutual. At least, not yet. Not so quickly. He was not free of the fear of commitment.

*　*　*

Fate has a way of stepping in when you need a helping hand. The movie Charles was working on was due to wrap in about a week. He decided he would call Christine then . . . give his mind a chance to 'unmuddle' itself. Several days before the final takes, the leading lady, Lila Turner, announced that the cast and crew were invited for 'cocktails and' in her dressing room after the final shoot.

On the way home, Charles considered the possibility of inviting Christine to escort him to the party. She would get a kick out of what a star's dressing room is like, not to mention all the celebs that would be there. He figured Christine was kind of star struck. And, she sure would look good on his arm. In spite of the little voice that cautioned, he decided to make the call. "To hell with you," he growled. "I'm gonna go for it." With that he had a quick something to eat, showered, and jumped into bed. He felt satisfied with himself for a change. Who knows? His decision might alter his drab life.

Since the divorce, he had avoided any personal changes in his raison d'etre. Socially, he was like a hermit crab who only emerged when necessary. Maybe now, as Jim says, I'll live a little. Okay, all you have to do now is make the call.

With this new perspective, he fell sound asleep. For a change, there was a smile upon his face.

CHAPTER THREE

The last few days on the set were hectic. Everyone was determined to finish on schedule. Some of the actors already had contracts for other gigs. Charles had been approached to do camera work on a planned blockbuster to be filmed on location—as yet, not determined. Filming went along smoothly and unless something unforeseen happened, they would close on schedule.

The Sunday before the planned cast party, Charles made the call. "Hi, Christine, how are you?"

Caught off guard, she asked, "Who is this?" but somehow she knew even before he answered.

"It's me, Charles, remember? Irish Pub . . . my friend Jim . . ."

"Oh, sure. That was a fun night."

Charles hesitated then nervously answered, "Fun, right. Lots of fun . . ." He hesitated. "I told you I'd call, so here I am." God, this was awkward. He should have rehearsed some repartee with Jim.

"So how have you been, Charles? Busy?"

"Busy, yes, but the movie's almost a wrap." He took a deep breath. "Say, Christine, the leading lady, Lila Turner, is throwing a cast and crew party when we finish. Would you like to go?" He blurted out the question.

For a moment, she hesitated. He had taken his time calling her . . . Well, what the hell. "When exactly is this party? I do have some commitments."

"Oh." Charles was flustered. Shit, I can't handle this. Say something, idiot. "We're hoping to wrap on Friday but you know how things are . . .

a little goof and we're into another day or more. But, we expect to be on time . . . that is, on Friday. Party's going to start about six-thirty. Is that okay with you?"

She laughed coyly. "Well, you don't deserve me but Friday it is." What the hell, he's a nice enough guy, besides I am extremely attracted to him. Not to mention a party attended by Hollywood celebs—more than intriguing. She might be "discovered". Who knows? She laughed again. "What time should I be ready, Charles?"

He could not believe this was actually happening. He tried hard not to betray his feelings. If she knew how delirious he was, she'd think he was nuts. "Great, Christine, I'll call you again to confirm, but I should be picking you up about six o'clock. See you then."

He could hardly wait to tell Jim. Charles knew that his friend had given up on him when he didn't call Christine after the night they met. Well, won't this news rock his cradle!

*   *   *

Later that Saturday night, as usual, Jim appeared ready for beer and mundane conversation. When he opened the door, the smile on Charles' face was as wide as a circus clown's.

Jim made no comment. He swept past Charles to the refrigerator and extracted a cold beer. He was ready to plant himself in the armchair next to the couch. Looking at Charles, he was aware that the broad smile still lingered. "What are you grinning at? You look like a computer nerd who just discovered a new complex calculation made easy through the magic of technology." He laughed. "How's that for a commercial?"

"You're not going to believe . . ."

"Okay, so I won't believe . . . what?"

Almost in a falsetto, Charles shouted, "I did it. I called Christine and she's going with me to the cast party Lila Turner's throwing in her dressing room."

Jim put down his beer and wrapped an arm around Charles' shoulders. "You son-of-a gun, you really made the move. Good for you."

"Jim, I still can't believe it. I keep thinking it's all in my imagination."

"Tell me everything—but first get me another beer."

They spent the evening hashing and rehashing the potentials of this upcoming date. By midnight, and after enough beer, the scenario assumed the proportions of Shakespeare's Romeo and Juliet.

*   *   *

The last few days of shooting went well. Charles phoned her on Thursday night. "Hi, Christine. Everything's on sched, so far. Could you be ready tomorrow at six? I'll pick you up . . . and, if the party should be postponed for any reason, we'll have dinner somewhere special."

"Fine, Charles. I'm looking forward to it." She hesitated, expecting him to add something. Nothing forthcoming, she added, "Well, I guess I'll see you tomorrow."

"Yes, oh, sure." Say something. She's going to think you're a real loser. "So, Chris . . . may I call you Chris?"

"Sure, if I can call you Charlie."

"Sounds good to me. So, how've you been? I'm really looking forward to us getting together. You're going to love Ms. Turner's dressing room."

"I've never been in a star's dressing room. I can hardly wait, and Charlie, I am anxious to see you again. I think we'll really hit if off."

A flustered Charles replied, "We'll be great together, I know." He took a deep breath. "Sweet dreams, Chris. See you tomorrow." After he put down the phone, he emitted a loud, whooping sound—to hell with the neighbors. "I've got a date with an angel."

*   *   *

His cab pulled up in front of Christine's place at exactly six. She was already waiting. This was a plus. Most women love to be late. His ex never seemed to be ready on time. He always had to urge her . . . even beg her . . . to hurry. His ears still burned when he recalled the expletives she hurled at him. Get your brain in gear, Charles. A lovely vision stands before you. He stepped out of the cab and helped Christine into the back seat where he took her hand and kissed it lightly . . . a move that surprised both of them. "You are breathtaking, Christine."

"Why, Charlie, how gallant!"

The cab driver waited patiently for a destination. No problem. The meter's running.

Finally, Charles cleared his throat. "Driver, Lot #4 at Paramount, please." He turned to Christine. "Really, you look so beautiful. I don't deserve you but I'm glad you're here with me."

"Charlie, don't be silly. I'm here because I want to be. Stop selling yourself short. You're not only handsome but a great guy, as well."

Impulsively, he bent towards her and kissed her cheek. "I promise to behave." He kissed her again, this time full on the mouth.

"That's more like it, Charlie-baby."

He rested his head against the back of the seat. A faint smile of satisfaction played about his lips. There's hope for me yet, he told himself.

Most of the cast and crew were already at the party when they arrived. Charles received a warm welcome, but eyes were on the stunning woman at his side. He introduced her all around and then took her on a tour of the dressing room. More like a small residence, there was a fully equipped bathroom, a make-up and dressing area, and a beautiful living room. It was furnished with a stunning white marble fireplace, white couches and chairs, all accented by exquisite accessories. The floor was covered with a plush, white rug.

Christine gasped in amazement. "My God, Charlie, this is spectacular. What a way to go!"

"Now, how about a visit to the bar?" Charles led the way. He ordered his usual beer. Christine opted for a vodka martini. As they circulated among the guests, they munched on Swedish meatballs and shrimp canapés. Charles enjoyed introducing her to the "in" people and watching her reaction. He could tell she was flabbergasted being in the company of so many top honchos in the film industry.

"This is so thrilling, Charlie. Thank you for inviting me. Meeting all these famous people, I'm just overwhelmed." She had a faraway look in her eyes. "And yet, somehow I feel this is where I belong." Christine closed her eyes for a brief moment and then flashed a brilliant smile at Charles. "You must think I'm conceited but this is my dream."

"I don't know about talent, but you certainly are the best looking gal in the place—or, anyplace, as far as I'm concerned."

"You're sweet. Let's have another drink."

Soft, romantic music added to the ambience. A few couples were slow dancing. Christine insisted upon joining them. Charles tried to resist. He was feeling high and afraid to get too close. Finally, she pulled him into her arms and they swayed to a popular love song, as Christine rubbed her cheek against his, holding him close. Old familiar feelings, suppressed for so long, surfaced as Charles did battle with his libido. As he was thinking about not thinking about it, a loud, unpleasant voice interrupted his train of thought.

"Well, hello Christine. It's been a long time, Baby."

"Not long enough, Blake."

Charles turned around to see who it was she had called Blake. Not a bad looking guy.

Blake's eyes, focused on Christine, flashed unpleasantly. "Come on, Baby. No need to be angry. I went away like a good boy when you told me to. It's been quite a while . . . thought maybe you'd be missing me."

"I didn't and I don't. Bug off." Christine turned her back to him. "Come on, Charlie, let's finish our dance."

He steered her to the other side of the room. "Who was that creep?"

"Creep is too nice a word for him. He sure had me fooled. We dated a few times and then he showed his true colors. He's nothing but a free-loading lounge lizard bit player. On our third date, I slapped his lying face and told him to get lost."

Charles interjected, "I don't like the way he looked at you. There was something evil in that twisted smirk."

"You got that right. The jerk stalked me for months until I threatened to go to the police. I knew he had a previous record . . . something about a DUI, I don't know. I really should have filed a complaint but, foolishly, I felt bad about doing it. Recently, I heard he latched on to some gal working at the Martinique. Boy, was I sorry for her. She's in for a rough time with that egomaniac."

Neither of them observed Blake's reddened face, the muscles twitching with consternation, his teeth locked into a grimace as he watched them from across the room. They danced over to the bar, ordered another drink and exchanged conversation with some guests nearby.

Blake's sudden exit wasn't even noticed.

The night seemed to fly by. Christine couldn't stop gushing about the "in" crowd. The director, John Victor, showed an interest in Christine and said something about a screen test . . . he would set it up with Charles, if she was interested. Interested? She was ecstatic.

By 2 a.m. most of the guests had departed. Charles wished their hostess good luck in her next role. She graciously kissed both of them, wishing them well. The evening had been perfect. Forgotten was the momentary unpleasantness of Blake's appearance.

Down at the gate, Charles hailed a cab in the deserted street and soon they arrived at Christine's apartment.

"Would you care for a night cap, or perhaps a cup of coffee?" She didn't want the evening to end.

Charles would have liked nothing better but he was afraid to destroy any gains he had made. Better go slow. "Thanks, Chris, but it is rather late and we've both had too much to drink." He regretted the words as soon as they spilled out of his mouth. He could tell she felt turned on.

Charles stammered, "It's not that I don't want to be with you, Chris. Believe me, I want nothing more, but I want it to happen under different circumstances . . . when we haven't been drinking so much."

"Drinking has nothing to do with it. I've been attracted to you from the first night I met you at the Pub. I thought you felt the same way . . ."

"Believe me, Chris, I do. Please be patient with me. I feel like such a fool. I haven't felt love for anyone in a long time but I know I could easily feel that way about you. That's why I want it to happen the right way."

"Charlie, what better way could there be?"

"Cold sober."

Christine was not about to press the matter any further. She understood where he was coming from and respected him for that and cared enough to play it his way. "Okay, sweet Charlie, what's our next move?"

"Dinner on Sunday?"

"You betcha!"

*   *   *

Charles did not sleep well. He kept thinking about Blake. Somehow, he sensed the potential for trouble.

The next morning, he awakened slowly. Suddenly, he bolted upright in bed. Jesus, why hadn't he realized this right away? How in hell did Blake gain entry to Lila's party? It was by invitation only. No one seemed to have acknowledged his presence. Got to get over to the studio and ask some questions.

On the lot, he sought out one of the guards who had been on duty. "Hey, Mike, remember Ms. Turner's party last night?" Without waiting for an answer, he continued, "Do you recall some guy crashing? Tall guy, mustache, black hair—name's Blake . . ."

Mike cut in, "Blake, yeah, asked if you and Christine were there yet, that you had invited him . . ."

"Did he ask about me by name?"

"No, he said 'that cameraman and his date Christine' had invited him, so I figured I'd better let him through."

Charles was annoyed. "Didn't it seem strange to you that I hadn't left his name at the gate and that he didn't even know my name?"

The guard was becoming uneasy. He could sense Charles' irritation. "To tell you the truth, I recognized him as one of the bit players at the studio, so I just took it for granted he was okay. Anyway, he said he was invited." He became defensive.

Anyone could get past this fool. So much for tight security. Charles, now angry, said a hasty goodbye and left. As he walked through the studio gates, he had the weirdest feeling that someone had witnessed the whole scene.

Questions in his mind began piling up, not only about Blake's appearance but how did he know that Christine would be at that party with him . . . that he was a cameraman. Rethinking the events of the evening, he realized that Blake had not said one word to him. His remarks were all directed at Christine. He hadn't even acknowledged Charles' presence.

When he returned to his apartment, Charles called her. "Hi, Chris, how's it going? Any hangovers or loss of memory?" He laughed . . . but she did not. "What's up, Babe, you don't sound happy." So he wasn't the only one up tight.

"I'm not happy, Charlie. I'm worried. I was having a wonderful time at the party until that jerk showed up and ruined it all. He's bad news."

"Chris, I know we weren't supposed to see each other until tomorrow for dinner, but do you think we could get together this afternoon for a cup of coffee and conversation?"

"Sure, if you want to." She was aware of the stress in his voice.

"I've been asking questions on the lot. I'll tell you about it when we meet. That guy bodes trouble, I think."

"Sweetie, I don't think he'd dare . . ."

"Chris, I've got bad vibes. Meet me at Starbucks on Vine. Three o'clock okay?"

"You betcha."

*   *   *

Charles watched her approach. Even in broad daylight, she was something to behold. He couldn't believe his luck. She was not only gorgeous but great company. He sure as hell wasn't going to let anything hurt her.

Christine observed Charles' demeanor as she walked towards the coffee shop. He was smiling but it was a strained smile and she sensed his mood was a troubled one. "Hi, Darling, it's great to see you again so soon." She kissed him lightly on the cheek.

He returned the kiss and put an arm around her shoulders. "It's good to see you, too."

They sat sipping cappuccinos slowly while Charles related his conversation with the studio guard. Christine was surprised at the way Blake had wheedled his way into the party.

Charles asked her, "Was there anything you may have told someone about our date that night that could have gotten back to Blake?"

Christine was certain. "I didn't speak to anyone about it."

"I don't understand how he knew you'd be there with me and that I'm a cameraman. Think hard, Chris. Were you anywhere recently where you might have mentioned the party? You know, you were pretty excited about it."

Chris raised her hand. "Oh, Charlie, wait a minute. I'm sorry. I just remembered . . . when I was at the beauty salon getting a manicure, I overheard one of the women mention she had heard rumors of a big bash planned in one of the star's dressing rooms at Paramount. I couldn't help but ask if she was referring to Ms. Turner's dressing room. She asked me how I knew about it. Oh, my God, that's when I said I had been invited by one of the cameramen . . .

"Then she gave me a peculiar look and buried her face in one of the magazines while her hairdresser continued to blow dry her hair. I don't know who she is, Charlie. I'm so sorry. I could try to find out who she is, I suppose, and if she has any connection to Blake."

"Darling, please do that. I'm on a mission now. I'll see you tomorrow as planned." On impulse, he kissed her lightly on the lips. This was another giant step for him.

Christine loved it. She kissed him back, hard.

They parted and Charles hurried back to his apartment. On the way home, he picked up a couple of six packs and some pretzels and a frozen dinner. If things progress with Christine the way he hoped then it would warrant a new arrangement with Jim.

Jim arrived earlier than usual. Charles had barely finished his dinner. "Hey, old pal, I could hardly wait to hear all about the big date." Jim reached for a beer out of the fridge.

Charles was a little put off. "Hey, just relax. Let me finish eating."

Jim sat down across the table from him. "I heard, via the grapevine, that it was some bash. One of the waiters told me about it. He eats breakfast at the same diner I do."

After they settled down with their beers in the living room, Charles related the events of the evening, including the incident with Blake.

"Did you say anything to the guy?" Jim asked.

"No. He didn't even look my way. He was so absorbed with Christine. She told him to bug off."

Jim was concerned. "Sounds like a bad dude. You've got to watch out for a guy like that. Doesn't take much for a stalker to go to the next level."

"Don't be an alarmist. This jerk's harmless. From what Christine tells me, the minute she threatened to report him, he faded from the scene." Charles did not want Jim to know how concerned he really was, so he didn't encourage further discussion. They spent the rest of the evening watching sports and polishing off another six pack.

*   *   *

Charles awoke late Sunday morning. All he wanted to think about was his date with Christine that evening. But, his thoughts kept reverting to Blake. He spent the afternoon straightening up. His usual Sunday chore. Taking a coffee break, he decided to call her.

She picked up the phone on the second ring. Her voice sounded irritated, as she answered, "I told you to stop calling me . . ."

"Chris, it's me. What's wrong?"

"Oh, Charlie," she sounded relieved, "that disgusting pig Blake has been harassing me again. Damn him!" Her voice became throaty and Charles could tell she was on the verge of tears.

"Chris, Baby, don't be upset. I'll get dressed and be right over."

An hour later, he arrived at her apartment. The door opened before he could ring the bell. Sobbing loudly, Christine threw herself into his arms. "Oh, Charlie, I'm so glad you're here. I've been miserable all day. That creep's been ringing me all morning."

"It's okay, Sweetheart. I'll always be here for you. Now, go wash your pretty face, put on a pretty dress and let's have a romantic dinner. I made reservations at Chasen's."

"You're so wonderful. How did I get so lucky?"

"I'm the lucky one. I never thought I could feel this way again." He took her into his arms.

She kissed him full mouth, pressing him close.

Charles was tempted to scratch the dinner plans but . . . no, don't hurry things. He gently pushed her away, reminding her that they would be late for their reservation.

She laughed. This guy's too much. "Well, I am hungry, but not necessarily for food." She tweaked the tip of his nose. "I'll be ready in a jiff. There's beer in the fridge."

A bottle of beer and a plush, comfortable chair relaxed him while he waited. When she reappeared, he sighed, "You are a dream come true."

Smiling radiantly, she teased, "But easy to resist, eh?"

Every part of Charles' body refuted her comment. "You must know that's no way true."

She did. But, he was calling the cards . . . and she was falling in love.

Candlelight, romantic music, and a fabulous meal plus the loving attention showered upon her made it a perfect evening for Christine. Temporarily forgotten was the specter of a stalking Blake. When they left the restaurant, there was no need to speak of where they were going. They knew they were going to bed.

Back in the apartment, Christine suggested a nightcap. "One drink, Darling, will not dull our senses . . ."

"Just one. All I want is to drink in your loveliness as I make love to you with a clear mind and all my heart." He realized how corny this must have sounded—but it was the truth.

She quickly poured two short scotch whiskies on-the-rocks. They toasted each other and gulped down the drinks. Charles took her into his arms, showering her with endearing terms and kisses as he ran his eager fingers over her body.

Christine responded with equal passion. As she explored his body, she moaned with pleasure. "Take me, Charlie. Now . . . please."

Lifting her into his arms, he carried her into the bedroom and gently laid her down upon the bed. As he hurriedly undressed, she removed her clothes. Whispering, "'Tis a consummation devoutly to be wished," he hungrily entered her. After a short, frantic first and then a prolonged encore, they both lay exhausted but happy. No need for words. At that moment all the stars in the Heavens were aligned and there was harmony in the Universe. Within minutes, two contented lovers were enveloped by deep sleep.

In the morning, Charles awoke to the aroma of bacon frying and coffee perking. He hesitated, thinking, "My God, it's not a dream." He found Christine in the kitchen preparing breakfast. Hugging her, her asked, "Did I die and go to Heaven?"

She laughed. "A good man deserves a good meal and **you are good.** Let's eat."

When they finished their meal, Christine suggested, "Why don't you shower and I'll do the dishes and catch up with you . . . in bed." There was temptation in her smile.

Charles rushed to the bathroom.

Soon, Christine was lying beside him. It was once more with feeling, as they say in show biz. However, the overtures of love making were short-lived, interrupted by the sharp jangle of the phone. "I rarely get calls this early in the morning. Oh, it better not be that creep!" The look on Christine's face had changed from anticipation to despair.

"Ignore it." Charles held her tightly.

"But, it may not be him. Could be a casting call. Better answer."

He released her reluctantly.

"Damn!" she shouted as she slammed down the phone.

"Shit! I can't believe that bastard is harassing you again. I'm calling the police." Charles reached for the phone.

"No, Charlie, please don't. You have no idea what a miserable, spiteful human being he is. He'll get away with it and then do something vengeful. I'm frightened."

He didn't say anymore but he promised himself that he would fix that S.O.B. Charles was fuming. It had been such a beautiful night and morning . . .

They spent the day quietly, watching TV and reading the papers. Dinner was ordered from a local restaurant and delivered. They ate in silence. Charles was shocked when Christine suddenly said, "Charlie, let's go to bed. I want to make love to you . . . to forget all about it."

"Are you sure? You seem so upset . . ."

"Charlie, I need you to love me. It's the only thing that will wipe out the memory of those awful calls."

He didn't need much more encouragement. There wasn't anything he'd rather do. He tried to make light of things. "You twisted my arm, Beautiful. Bed it is."

For an intensely gratifying hour or so, it was sheer delight.

Charles offered to stay the night, but Christine assured him she would be "just fine". "I'll call you if I need you."

"For sure? If anything at all happens to upset you, promise you'll call immediately."

"I promise."

*   *   *

At last, morning. Charles called Christine as soon as he awoke. "How are you? Did you get some sleep?"

"I'm okay, Charlie. Don't worry. I'll be fine." She didn't say that the phone rang twice late into the night. "How about you?"

"Well, if you call dozing off in the wee hours, sleep . . . Sweetheart, yesterday was wonderful. I'll call you later. Have a couple of things I have to do."

"Okay, Lover. I'll be here." Her lips made the sounds of a kiss.

"Right back at you." He hung up.

Charles decided as long as he had some time on his hands, he'd do some more sleuthing around the studio.

CHAPTER FOUR

Life is tough out in Hollywood. It's a who-you-know place, and if you know the right people, it greatly reduces the wear and tear.

By Monday afternoon, Charles was back at the studio intending to get some information on Blake when he ran into John Victor, the director who had been at Ms. Turner's party. It turned out to be a mutually convenient meeting.

"Charles, I'm glad to see you. I've been so damn busy . . . meant to call you about your friend—Christine, is it?"

"Yes, it is. Good to see you, too, Mr. V." (Everyone called him that.)

"Your girl's a looker, as we used to say, and if she has the talent to match, maybe we can do something with her. I've got a new film in the works. And, Charles, you know I always want you on camera."

"Thanks, Mr. V., I appreciate that and I know Christine will be grateful for your help."

"Call my office tomorrow a.m. My secretary will give you the info about the screen test. I'll set it up a.s.a.p. Tell Christine I said good luck."

Charles could hardly conceal the rush he was feeling. "I can't thank you enough."

"No need to."

They shook hands.

*   *   *

Charles couldn't wait to phone her. Right now Blake was the furthest from his mind. Catching a break like this in Hollywood was awesome.

Returning to his apartment, he dialed her number. When she didn't pick up right away, he was concerned. Then she answered, saying, "Yes?" and nothing more.

"Chris, Honey, it's me . . ."

"Oh, thank goodness." She sighed heavily and he sensed something was wrong. "Everything okay, Chris?"

"If you can call heavy breathing and three hang-ups okay . . ."

"That no good bum, again? Listen, Chris, I have some great news for you. Forget about Blake. I was at the studio today and met John Victor, the director. Remember him?"

"Sure do. Did he say anything about me?"

"Only that he's setting up a screen test for you. Is that fabulous, or what?"

Chris shrieked with delight. She couldn't verbalize the excitement coursing through her . . . only sound bites of gratitude, ending with, "Charlie-Baby, I love you with all my heart."

"And I, you. See you at seven for dinner?"

"You betcha!"

*   *   *

They opted for a casual meal at a local pizzeria on Vine. Christine had trouble concentrating on her food; she was overwhelmed by her good fortune. "It all happened because of you. I'd still be waiting for an "extra" casting call. I can't believe my luck. Thank you, thank you, thank you. I do love you, Charlie."

"You're welcome and I love you. Let's do something relaxing. How about a movie?"

Christine smiled demurely but there was nothing shy or coy about her answer. "There's only one thing that can relax me now . . . making crazy, mad love with you."

That suited Charles just fine.

Back at her apartment, they shed their clothes, piece by piece, as they stumbled to the bedroom, kissing ardently, frantically. By the time they threw themselves upon the bed, they were laughing uncontrollably. He kissed her face and ears and neck as he caressed her supple body. Their laughter had morphed into sighs and moans of pleasure. Her gasps of passion urged him on while her body responded in spasms to his slow, passionate movements.

They made love into the late hours until they fell apart, sweaty and exhausted. The curtain of night soon enveloped them.

In the morning, after a shower, coffee and toast, Charles kissed her softly on the forehead. "Got to go home, my love, to make that important call." He smiled sheepishly. "Mr. V.'s number is on my desk."

"Promise you'll call the minute you get any information."

"Of course I will, you know that."

"Charlie, you are like fine wine that improves with time." She squeezed him close for a moment and then shoved him out the door.

*   *   *

The secretary was quick and precise on the phone. "Christine is to report to Stage 4 on the Paramount lot, at 10 a.m., on the following Monday, September 17th. You are welcome to accompany her. Please call if a problem should arise. We will do likewise. Good luck."

Charles thanked her and immediately called Christine. "All set, Baby. Be prepared to become a new star in Hollywoodland. I'll give you the details when I see you."

For a moment, she didn't utter a word then the silence was broken by a loud, ear piercing, "Yes! Yes!"

"I thought women only shout like that when they climax. A screen test must be right up there with great sex, eh?"

She laughed. Then seriously, "Honey, this means so much to me and I have you to thank for it. How can I ever make this up to you?"

"Chris, when we make love, it's like we are a part of each other. I don't need anymore. See you tonight?"

"You got it . . . but, we're dining in, courtesy Chez Christine's. How does that grab you?"

"Super! I'll bring the fine wine."

*   *   *

The balance of the week passed slowly but pleasantly. Charles and Christine spent every evening together that week with the exception of Saturday night, Jim's night.

"I'm going to tell Jim that Saturday nights are off limits from now on because you and I are definitely 'a thing'."

She looked at him quizzically. "A thing?"

He quickly added, "I mean, we're together . . . very much in love . . . oh, you know what I mean. Saturday nights belong to us from now on."

"I hope Jim won't resent me."

"He's my best friend and a good guy. I'll just suggest another night . . . a week night. We'll be fine."

Truth be told, when Charles explained it to Jim, he felt bad about the change, but, he understood. "Hey, Charlie, I think I can still appreciate the feeling of wanting to be with a certain someone." He shrugged. "Christine rings your bell. I'm happy for you."

Charles slapped him on the back. "You're a pal. How about Tuesday or Thursday evenings. We can still go over to the Pub once in a while, if you like."

"Thursday's good. We'll just have to make it an early night, that's all. Friday's a work day. I'm not on vacation the way you are between films."

Charles laughed. "Come on. You've got the staff at the newspaper dancing around your schedule. You being a reporter, you don't exactly punch a clock."

"Okay, Sport. Thursdays it is . . . until you should decide you can't be away a single night."

Charles placed his hand on Jim's shoulder. "We're still good, eh?"

"The best."

*   *   *

Nothing could dampen Christine's spirits that week, not even Blake's hang-ups. She and Charles spent happy hours dining, loving, and sleeping in. Christine had missed his company on Saturday night but she was happy in the knowledge that it would be different next week and every week thereafter. They would have entire weekends together.

Sunday morning, she eagerly awaited him for breakfast. On the table, dishes were stacked with pancakes, sides of bacon, eggs and toasted muffins. Coffee perked on the sideboard. Christine had timed it so everything would be ready as soon as Charles arrived at ten o'clock. He was always prompt.

By ten-thirty, she was worried. This was not like him, not to call if he was delayed. She dialed his home phone. No answer. Finally, a call to his cell brought results. "Charlie, are you all right?"

"Chris, I'm sorry. I should have called you right away. When I got into my car, I didn't notice at first, but as I backed down the driveway, it became obvious that I had a flat. Called road service and they just finished. There was no nail or anything like that; it was strange, all the air was out of the tire."

"Charlie, do you think . . . ?"

"Darling, we can't blame Blake for everything that goes wrong. Shit happens. I'm on my way. See you in a few."

Christine had her own ideas about the flat.

So did Charles.

*   *   *

Breakfast was still tasty after a quick reheat in the toaster oven. Later, they got comfortable on the couch and browsed through the morning newspaper which he had picked up on his way. They read, watched TV, had dinner, and both agreed that a wild night was **not** in order.

"You've got to be rested and refreshed and beautiful for tomorrow's screen test. Early to bed, to sleep is definitely **in** order."

The next morning, as the guard waved them through the Paramount gate, Christine exclaimed, "I can't believe it's really happening. Charlie, you have no idea how I feel. This is something most actors dream about but never get the break. I'll give it my best shot and if it doesn't work out . . ."

"Chris, it will work out. You've got the brains, talent and beauty. Think positively."

"I'm trying, Baby, I'm trying."

Charles parked the car near Stage 4 and escorted her inside where they met with Mr. Victor who explained the character she was to portray and the circumstances. Acting opposite her would be one of Hollywood's leading men, Russ Crowell. Christine's eyes widened as she inhaled deeply.

Charles smiled at her. "Go for it!"

*   *   *

After watching the screen test the next day, Mr. V. called her in for an interview. The director's comments were reassuring about her future. "Darling, you are going to be the best thing that has happened to Hollywood in a long time—a leading lady of true star material."

Turning to Charles, he said, "What a great find, my boy." Then, to Christine, "Get an agent, Sweetheart. I've shown the rushes to a couple of producers and they are willing to give you a contract on the basis of your screen test. I'll have you back here as soon as the papers are drawn up. If we shake hands on it, we'll get to work on a PR campaign and set this town on fire." He wrapped his arms around her. "Darling, we will work wonders together. It won't be long before you'll be leaving your footprints in cement at Grauman's Chinese Theatre."

"Oh, Mr. Victor, thank you so much for your confidence in me."

"My dear, I know real talent and beauty when I see it."

Mr. V. turned to Charles. "My boy, we've got pure gold here."

Charles had no argument with that.

On the way to the car, Christine couldn't stop gushing. "Oh, my God, it's my dream come true." She stopped to take a deep breath and to kiss Charles. "I hope I live up to everybody's expectations."

"Chris, remember it's all about self-confidence." He hugged her. "You're adorable and I'm so happy for you. From now on you've got to start acting like a star. Wait until the story breaks. You're in for one helluva ride!"

"Right now, I'm so excited. I want to feel this way for a little while until I get it out of my system and calm down—if I ever do."

"Okay. Let's go celebrate. How about lunch at Martinique's?"

"Swell." She giggled. "Where did that word come from?"

"Watching too many old movies."

At the restaurant, they were seated near the windows, with Charles facing the dining room, Christine with her back to it. A solicitous waiter took their orders and quickly returned with their cocktails. (The help always assumed they were serving the "in" people. Many waiters were hopefuls and wannabes themselves, longing to be discovered.)

Neither Christine nor Charles thought of the significance of Martinique's until he glanced across the room toward the entrance. There at the desk stood a most unwelcome sight. Blake, who apparently had some connection with the hostess. Their familiarity was evident by the way he whispered in her ear and their low laughter. Charles realized this must be the girl from the beauty parlor that Christine had referenced. He was glad that Christine was not aware of Blake's presence. Seeing him would ruin her day. Why had he suggested this place?

Lifting his glass to toast the occasion, Charles glanced across the room. The smirk on Blake's face infuriated him but he quickly looked back at Christine's radiant face and leaned across the table to kiss her. "To a new star in Movieland's galaxy."

Her eyes sparkled with happiness. "To us, Sweetheart."

Charles silently vowed that he would never let anyone harm her. "Darling, I love you with all my heart, for sure."

He was also sure of something else. He had learned a little more about Blake's sphere of activity.

CHAPTER FIVE

Charles was acquainted with several reputable agents in town. He decided to call Jack Murdock because he knew he did well with new faces. "Hello, Jack, this is Charles Markham. We met on the Paramount set of LOVE IN PARADISE earlier this year when I was on camera.

"Yes, I remember you. How've you been, Charles? What can I do for you?"

Charles took a deep breath. "John Victor's excited about a new find . . . happens to be my girl friend Christine. After she tested, he was so impressed he suggested she get an agent. The producers of his upcoming film are willing to sign a contract with her based on that test. Would you be interested in representing Christine?"

"I usually don't work sight unseen, but Mr. V. has a reputation for picking winners. Tell you what . . . let's get together for coffee and we'll take it from there. How about tomorrow morning, ten o'clock, my office?"

"Thanks, Mr. Murdock. I really appreciate this. You won't regret it. Tomorrow at ten."

"I'm anxious to meet your Christine. Look forward to tomorrow." He hung up.

Charles was overjoyed. He hadn't known what to expect. Jack Murdock had an impressive and impeccable reputation as a star maker and was known to drive a hard bargain in contract negotiations. It would be nothing short of fantastic if he agreed to represent Christine.

*   *   *

When Christine opened her door, Charles grabbed her, kissed her and began to whirl her around the apartment.

"What? What is it?" she asked.

"Sweetheart, if all goes well, you will be represented by one of the sharpest agents in the movie business."

Christine was breathless. "Charlie, stop dancing and tell me—who are you talking about?"

"Jack Murdock! One of the best. We have a meeting with him tomorrow morning at his office. How about that?"

"I can't believe it! My love, you are making it all happen. I will be forever grateful to you."

He pulled her close. "How about a little gratitude right now?"

"You betcha."

*   *   *

It was still dark out when Charles woke up suddenly and found himself alone in bed. "Chris, where are you?"

"Charlie, go back to sleep. I need some extra time for beauty repairs. The shape I'm in right now, I'd never pass muster." She laughed at herself.

He laughed, too. "Okay, just give me a wake-up call about forty-five minutes before we have to leave. I could use a little restoration myself."

Christine showered, shampooed and blow-dried her lovely, long auburn hair. She chose to wear a print dress of soft chiffon which accented her figure and emphasized the crystal clear green of her eyes.

Charles quickly showered, shaved and dressed. When he joined her in the living room, he stood for a moment appraising her. "You are a vision to behold. Too bad we can't afford to miss this meeting . . . I'd make a proposition you couldn't refuse. Chris, you are irresistible."

She giggled and took his arm. "Come on, Charlie, let's get going. I can hardly wait to meet Jack Murdock."

He bowed gallantly and ushered her out the door. First things first.

When they entered his office, Jack Murdock was immediately aware that the beauty on Charles' arm was something special. For a moment, he glanced at Charles and couldn't help but wonder why he had never considered working in front of the cameras. So handsome . . . and the timbre of his voice was so fine. Murdock turned his eyes back to Christine.

"Mr. Murdock, this is Christine O'Hara." Charles was beaming.

"Christine, my dear, so good to meet you . . . and to see you, too, Charles. Let's have our coffee and chat." He rang for his secretary who soon appeared with a tray carrying coffee and croissants. Murdock spoke, in general, about actors, studios, and contracts. He then zeroed in on specifics: What were Christine's expectations and ideas about her career? As her agent, he explained what his contractual demands would be and exactly in what matters he would represent her.

Christine found it all mind-boggling. After much discussion, they signed a contract and shook hands on it. Once more Murdock rang for his secretary. Either she was clairvoyant or Murdock had assumed that their meeting would result in a signed contract. She appeared with three flutes and a bottle of fine champagne.

Christine's eyes widened in surprise. Charles gave her a look that said, Get used to this. It's only the beginning.

They each took a glass and Murdock lifted his, saying, "To you, my dear. I wish you success and happiness. Enjoy the dream."

Glasses clinked. Christine was overcome with emotion. Her "thank you" was barely audible. Her voice caught in her throat and her eyes shone with tears of joy.

Murdock gave her a hug. "Give me a call when Mr. V. tells you they are ready to discuss the contract. Good luck."

Christine nodded in agreement. "Thank you so much. I'll call as soon as I hear anything."

*   *   *

Within a week, they were all sitting around a conference table in Mr. V.'s office. Present were Charles, Christine, Jack Murdock, two producers and their attorneys. After much discussion and maneuvering, they finally settled upon a mutually acceptable contract. There was hand shaking and hugging and pats on the back, and, of course, champagne for everyone.

Mr. V. excused himself for a moment. "I have a call to make."

The others chatted while he did so.

"All right," Mr. V. announced, "now we are all going to Martinique's. I've made reservations. Drink up!"

Martinique's! Charles dreaded going there again. But, how could he tell Mr. V. about Christine's problem? All Charles could hope for was that Blake would be nowhere in sight.

When they arrived at the restaurant, they stopped at the hostess' desk. As they stood there waiting to be seated, Christine suddenly pulled

Charles aside, whispering, "The hostess is the woman I told you about in the beauty parlor . . . the one who mentioned the party, remember?"

"Sure, Honey, but let's not bother with that. We're here to celebrate your new contract and your new life."

"You're right." She smiled up at him.

Charles did not show the consternation he felt. Of all the places, on this happy day, why did they have to be reminded of unpleasantness. He wondered if the hostess recognized Christine. The last thing he wanted was an appearance by Blake. My girl is radiant with happiness and I want it to stay that way.

As always, prominent people were seated where they could be seen, unless they requested otherwise. Mr. V. had arranged for a large, round, center table upon which an elaborate bouquet of flowers awaited Christine. In Hollywood, the key word is flamboyance. Christine was in awe of all the attention. There must have been some advance PR because there was even applause from some of the other tables.

Christine was overwhelmed as she clung to Charles' arm. "Oh, my God, Charlie . . ."

"It's all for you, Baby. Go for it!"

She lit up the table with her smile. It was a magical time. They dined and drank more champagne. Everyone was on a high. It was a Hollywood event filled with dreams of stardom, Oscars, and big money.

For Christine, it was a dream come true. She would have signed the contract without a thought about the money. Leaning close to Charles, she whispered, "This is the best day of my life . . . besides the day I met you, my love."

*   *   *

Christine's life became a whirlwind of activity from the moment she received the call from Casting. She was deluged with appointments with make-up artists, hair designers, and voice and diction coaches. The many demands upon her allowed her little spare time and, most evenings, she was exhausted. One night, she fell asleep in Charles' arms in the middle of a conversation. She awoke and said, apologetically,

"I'm sorry, Honey, but they've got me on a merry-go-round."

"Chris, I love you. Don't worry about it. I'm happy to be with you, asleep or otherwise."

"I can hardly wait for casting to be completed and a shooting schedule set up."

"Chris, you'll have a breathing spell soon between Thanksgiving and New Year's. The industry usually slows down during that time," he assured her. "Relax, Honey, this is all new to you now. Naturally, you get up tight once in a while. Remember, everyone is showing confidence in you. Now you have to show them they're right." He kissed her on the forehead.

"Charlie, what would I do without you? You're so good for me." She sighed deeply. "I feel better now."

"Come closer and I'll make you feel even better."

She slid into his arms and, for awhile, neither gave any thought to her seven a.m. studio call. All that mattered was their intense desire. They made love as though it was the first time. Afterwards, they lay there, breathing heavily and smiling contentedly. Even the insistent ringing of the phone could not disturb the mood.

Charles had solved the unwanted phone call problem by buying Christine an I.D. Now she could answer only when she wished to. The answering machine was on 'off'. Tonight, they both glanced at it and enjoyed a good laugh. The arrogant, sneering voice was no more. If only it were that easy to eliminate his presence.

*　　*　　*

The days flew by and, more and more, Christine adapted to the life of a movie actor. As the holidays approached and the business of making movies went into slow motion, there were endless cocktail hours and parties to which she and Charles were invited. They were easily caught up in the celebratory activities.

One night, in particular, when they were due at Mr. V.'s estate in town, they became aware that they were being followed. Charles wanted to stop the car and confront the driver.

"Please, Charlie, don't. We don't know who it is. It could be the paparazzi. And, if it is Blake, then it's best we ignore him. He's got a terrible temper and is obviously looking for trouble."

"Christine, I don't know how much longer we can overlook his shenanigans. We've got to do something about his harassment."

We're almost at Mr. V.'s. Let's just keep going . . ."

"If you insist. I don't want to upset you, but, I tell you, we're going to have to do something about him."

When they pulled into the driveway, Charles noticed that the car behind them slowed down and then sped away. He said nothing. Why do people do stupid things? He turned to Christine and gave her a big kiss. "You are gorgeous and we are going to have the time of our lives tonight."

She laughed and kissed him back. "You betcha!"

Everybody who was anybody in Hollywood was at the party. Mr. V. took a personal interest in introducing Christine. Clinking upon his glass, he asked for attention, got it and then announced: "Let me introduce Christine O'Hara, a new talent in the Paramount family. Some of you have already met her. Please make her welcome."

A rousing applause followed. Christine, mustering all her self-assurance, smiled and demurely thanked Mr. V. and his distinguished guests. "I am happy to be a member of the motion picture industry," brought more applause.

Mr. V. hugged her and urged, "Drink up and enjoy the wonderful catering of the Belle Maison." He lifted his glass. "To the longevity of motion pictures."

The happy couple circulated and enjoyed chit-chat with some of the guests who were working actors Christine had watched on the screen for many years.

"Oh, Charlie, what a fabulous night! I can't believe this is really happening."

After a few drinks and hors d'oeuvres, they decided they'd better get some real food down before doing any more drinking. Charles teased her. "I wouldn't want you to act silly or anything."

"Silly? No, but I might start acting sexy . . . being here with you and so happy . . . I could climb right up your tempting body."

"I'll look forward to that when we get back to the apartment. Right now, make like a movie star and rack up some points with your fellow thespians."

She pouted then smiled mischievously. "Okay, but you'd better gird your loins for later combat."

Charles laughed. "I'll be ready," he promised.

The rest of the evening was typically Hollywood. A lot of chit chat, dissing, who's in, who's out . . .

There were streaks of dawn across the sky by the time Charles and Christine said their goodbyes and headed home. Despite the long night, she was not deterred from fulfilling her 'threat'. As soon as they closed the door, Christine kicked off her shoes, shed her gown and asked, "Are you ready for this?" Without waiting for an answer, she sprang at Charles, wrapped her legs around his waist and locked her arms around his neck.

It took only a moment for Charles to catch his breath and become revitalized. "Sweetheart, you missed your vocation—you're a bloody acrobat!"

"Hold tight, you're in for a swinging time."

*   *   *

The next day, Christine said, "Charlie, with all these invitations, I've got to do some serious work on my wardrobe. You know what they say about getting caught wearing the same thing twice."

"Darling, the only thing people will notice is how beautiful you are."

"You're prejudiced. You know how important the right wardrobe is in Tinsel Town. They'll take notice right down to my toe nails."

"Okay, I'm convinced. Let's go shopping. I'll call for a cab."

Christine did a quick survey in the nearest mirror, added some lipstick and ran a comb through her hair. She grabbed her purse. "This is so exciting!"

Charles suggested, "Let's go to the Hollywood Woman on Rodeo Drive. The place is known for unique outfits and accessories for women of the silver screen . . . and wannabes who can afford to shop there."

"Great suggestion. I can hardly wait."

Downstairs, a cabby honked his horn.

Charles and Christine quickly headed for the elevator.

Within a short while, they arrived at the Hollywood Woman. Once inside, the selections of gold and silver threaded chiffons, jeweled satins, exotic silks and sleek leathers overwhelmed Christine. She was like a child in a candy store. "Oh, look, isn't it gorgeous?" she asked, as she flitted from one mannequin to another. She continued to exclaim her satisfaction as she examined every rack. By the time she got to the accessories, her eyes were dancing in her head.

Charles put an arm around her. "Time to make decisions. What do you think about three cocktail outfits and three dinner gowns, for starters? With accessories to match, of course. And, it's all a gift from me."

"Oh, Charlie, it sounds wonderful . . . but I can't let you do this . . ."

"Yes, you can. Besides, I want to be able to brag that I dressed you before you became a star."

Right there in the middle of the store, she impulsively hugged and kissed him.

They asked for a saleslady's assistance and after a few hours of trying on, fittings, and picking out the appropriate accessories, Christine left instructions for their delivery.

The happy pair walked out into the bright sunlight. Charles suggested, "Let's have a cappuccino to celebrate. You look like you need to catch your breath."

"Great idea. Later, I want to feel breathless again. I want to show you how good you are for me."

Charles reached for her but at that moment a familiar, unwelcome voice pierced the air. "Well, well, if it isn't the great Lillian Gish of our day."

Christine and Charles spun around to face Blake. Christine shuddered.

Charles demanded, "What the hell do you want? You're asking for trouble."

Blake shrugged. "What's your problem? I just happened to be passing by. I only want to wish our girl good luck."

"She's not **our** girl, she's **my** girl and the next time I find you anywhere near her or annoying her in any way, you're history."

Blake shook his head; his face showed mock concern. "You shouldn't get so excited. Bad for the heart."

Charles clenched his fists and would have slammed one into Blake's jaw if Christine hadn't grabbed his arm. "Please, Charlie, let's just get away from here."

He could see that she was about to cry. "Okay, Sweetheart." He turned to Blake. "One of these days, you'll get what you deserve."

"Yes, I'm sure I will . . . and won't you be surprised."

Blake's outrageous attitude rankled Charles but he turned his attention to Christine. Comforting her, he led her away and hailed a cab.

Neither one of them looked back to see the expression of pure malice on Blake's face.

Chapter Six

Blake Dugan, growing up in New York City's Hell's Kitchen, was better looking than most of his peers—and he had ambition. Women adored him, even though he often mistreated them; men admired but often feared him. Blake had a brashness about him, a bravado that carried him through tough circumstances; he was no stranger to trouble.

His good looks and conceit fostered an interest in acting. Blake welcomed all the attention he could get. When the drama coach in his high school invited him to join the Drama Club, he jumped at the chance. He loved the rush he got every time he was on stage. After graduation, he opted for a career in the theatre. Much to his dismay, he was unsuccessful and, after several years, he decided to head out to Hollywood where, he heard, it might be easier to be discovered. That myth soon evaporated.

Desperate for more money than he earned from odd and demeaning jobs, he got involved with some unsavory characters on Sunset Strip, one of the toughest streets in the town and the heart of Hollywood vice. There he was approached by a man who offered him a job as an escort. "Here's my card. Give me a call."

It didn't take long for Blake Dugan to become one of Hollywood's most sought after escorts.

He juggled the hours between his nightlife and daytime commitments—visiting casting offices, still following his aspirations. There were occasions when he escorted connected film people, always sure to tell them of his ambition. Much to his chagrin, there were no takers and he had to content himself with a now-and-then part as an extra.

Blake met Christine one evening at a popular Hollywood club. The actress he was escorting was acquainted with Christine and introduced them. Immediately, he focused his attention on Christine, much to his date's annoyance.

"Listen, Buster," she said angrily, "I'm not paying for your company so you can find someone else to fall over."

Blake gave her a scathing look. "If you're not happy, leave. You won't be billed."

Before she stomped away, she told a stunned Christine, "Good luck with that loser."

Blake was his charming best, explaining away his date's early departure as a fit of jealousy. That evening led to a series of dates with Christine. With each one, she became more and more disillusioned. Blake was nothing he purported to be. Soon, he became an albatross around her neck, possessive and demanding.

One night, over a drink, Christine said, "Blake I don't think we should see each other anymore. I can't be what you obviously want and I don't share your feelings."

"Christine, don't say that. You are everything I want in a woman. Just give it time and you'll feel the same way I do."

"I'm sorry . . . I'm afraid not . . ."

His face reddened. "You're no different from all those Hollywood two-bit players!" His voice rose. "Go ahead, Miss Wonderful, see if you can do better."

"Blake, please, I didn't intend for us to argue. Be reasonable. You're embarrassing me . . ."

"Reasonable? You bitch!"

Christine stood up. "Goodbye, Blake." She exited quickly.

What followed were endless phone calls, snide remarks and sudden appearances in public places as Blake continued to stalk her. When he learned of her relationship with Charles, the flames of envy stoked into a four-alarm blaze.

*　　*　　*

After Charles and Christine's encounter with Blake in front of the Hollywood Woman, Charles decided to do a background check on him. He said nothing to Christine. She was excited about her blossoming career. Her first film, THE FLAWLESS MISTRESS, was scheduled to begin shooting within two weeks. Casting was complete except for some extras.

The first shoot was set. Cast and crew were ready at seven a.m. The director called "places". The scene: A huge ballroom, couples in period costume, dancing to a Strauss waltz, extras milling about. Christine stood in place; Russ Crowell stood facing her.

Charles, on camera, scanned the room and adjusted his lens accordingly for a long shot. Suddenly, he saw a familiar, disturbing figure. Blake! How in hell had he gotten in as an extra? He wondered if Christine had noticed him. Would her performance be affected?

Mr. V. called, "Lights, camera, action."

The shoot went smoothly. "It's a take" was heard often. Charles didn't have an opportunity to speak with Christine between scenes because she was either in wardrobe or make-up. He gradually assumed that Christine was not aware of Blake. He didn't realize how wrong he was until they were at her apartment that evening.

"Charlie, in case you are wondering and concerned, I did notice Blake but I am not going to let him spoil this for me."

"I'm so relieved, Chris. It troubled me all day. I don't want anything to ruin your happiness. I'm so proud of you. You were just great on the set. A natural."

They kissed. Charles filled glasses with champagne. "To the first day of a long and successful career, Darling."

"There's only one thing that can improve upon this day."

*   *   *

The next day, Charles made a call. "Hi, Jim, I need a favor."

"Hey, long time no see. What kind of favor?"

"Remember that character I told you about—the one stalking Christine?"

"Yeah. Don't tell me he's still at it."

"Yes. I want some info on this guy. He's no amateur. Nervy bastard, turns up everywhere. Makes irritating comments. Now for the last straw, he's an extra in Christine's film."

"You're kidding! How did he wrangle that?"

"Either dumb luck or he's got a connection."

"Well, he can't be too well connected if all he can get is extra work. What is it you need from me?"

"A background check on the creep. You once mentioned that you've got some friends who do that sort of thing. Can you help?"

"Tell me what you know and I'll handle the rest."

"Thanks, Jim. I appreciate it."

They spoke for a while. Jim reassured him, "I'll get back a.s.a.p."

*　　*　　*

Shooting was on mark. Several days passed without incident. Christine and Charles spent most evenings at her place, stopping occasionally for a sentimental drink at the Pub. On one such night, Charles told her, "You realize, Chris, that once the PR is stepped up for FLAWLESS MISTRESS, it's going to be difficult to drop in at the Pub for a casual drink."

"You think? I mean, what could be bad about doing that?"

"People hounding you, not to mention the paparazzi who can be a pain in the butt, at times. You're going to have to pick and choose your public appearances carefully. It becomes a question of where you <u>have</u> to go, not always where you <u>want</u> to go. Not easy."

"Charlie, we'll make it work, whatever it takes. Now, let's get a good night's sleep. I have a seven a.m. make-up and wardrobe call. As you know, we're shooting the final scene out of sequence and I have to look ravishing." She laughed.

"You always do. Not to worry."

They kissed, rolled over on their sides and fell fast asleep.

A late night call woke Charles. He grabbed the phone quickly while checking the caller ID. He glanced toward Christine. Luckily, she had not been disturbed. Good. He picked up the phone, speaking softly, "Hello, Jim."

"Hey, sorry to call so late but I've got some dirt. Can we meet for coffee early a.m. tomorrow? I've got to be at the paper by eight-thirty for a meeting."

"Sure. Great. Christine has a seven o'clock call. That gives me about an hour or so before I get behind the camera. Meet me at the commissary on the lot. I'll leave your name at the gate."

The next morning, after leaving Christine on the set, Charles headed for his meeting with Jim.

They shook hands. "Can't tell you how much I appreciate this."

"No need to," Jim said. "Just remember me when Christine grants interviews," he teased.

Charles answered seriously, "You can depend on it."

"Well, I won't hold you to it, so don't worry. I know the routine. Anyway, let's get down to the bare facts about Blake. Seems he racked up a record in New York . . . couple of DUI's and some stalking charges. The lucky s.o.b. got off lightly the first time by doing public service. Second time, he served a few days. Stalking charges were filed but somehow he never got more than a slap on the wrist. However, from what I hear, he's well known to the police. He was a person of interest in a couple of drug busts but apparently was able to clear himself. He's been a bad boy in the big City."

"Blake better watch his step. If he does anything to harm Christine . . ."

"Take it easy, Charles. Don't do anything foolish."

"Don't worry, Jim. Foolish, I'm not, but I am determined to destroy him."

"Be careful, my friend. I'd hate to see you get into trouble."

"I'm cool. Not to worry. Now I've got to get behind the camera." Charles shook Jim's hand and patted him on the back. "Thanks, again. I owe you."

When Charles returned to the set, it was in turmoil. Immediately, his eyes searched for Christine. At first, he didn't notice her then he realized she was in the center of a group of cast members—and she was crying.

"Christine, what's wrong?"

"Oh, Charlie, someone trashed my dressing room . . ."

"What the hell!" He rushed over to her trailer. Everything was in disarray. Her sides of the script were scattered all over. The place was a mess. Charles was fuming. So much time would be lost retrieving the script and getting things back in order. No need to wonder who did this. Charles knew but how could he prove it.

Mr. V. was outraged. The palpable question was should the police be called. That call would cost a day of shooting, at least. Mr. V. made the call. The culprit had to be found.

The police asked questions, investigated the scene, and gathered whatever could be used as evidence. They questioned Charles. He didn't hesitate to voice his suspicions. The officers made note of it.

On the way home, Charles tried hard to comfort a distraught Christine. "A whole day of shooting wasted . . . and my things . . . my script. Oh, Charlie, I feel so responsible. Maybe I should ask Mr. V. if he'd like to replace me. Who knows what else will happen? We're dealing with a loose canon. God only knows what that idiot Blake will do next."

"Chris, no way will I let this destroy you and your career. I promise you, I'll make things right."

The night seemed endless to both of them as they sat in the kitchen. They drank one cup of coffee after another as the clock moved relentlessly past midnight. Finally, they went to bed. Christine succumbed to fatigue but Charles watched the sky lighten as morning approached.

He was ready to reduce Blake to ruin.

CHAPTER SEVEN

M r. V. has the reputation for being a meticulous and creative director. Some directors work closely with their actors, outlining every move, analyzing each bit of dialogue even to the slightest nuance. Mr. V. tended to give his actors more reign. He would briefly describe what he hoped to achieve in each scene and then expected that the actors would add their own instinctive touches. His adroitness usually elicited fine results.

Except for the unfortunate incident regarding Christine's trailer, shooting was going well. So far, no evidence had been found to incriminate anyone—much to Charles' angst.

Finances are always of the essence, so both producers and director were happy they were shooting on schedule. Christine and Russ worked well together. There was an electricity between them that spelled big box office. When they rehearsed scenes and all went well, Mr. V. knew that would translate onto the screen. "Don't ask me why," he would say. "It's a mystery I don't understand, but such is the fact."

Christine occasionally sat in on the evening rushes (dailies) even though, as most actors are wont to be, she was nervous about watching them. It was a learning experience for her regarding lighting, camera angles, make-up and seeing herself in character. Charles was always there, cheering her on. For Mr. V. and crew, it was a way of detecting technical flaws or scenes that did not jell and would require retakes. Luckily, there weren't too many. His positive assessment inspired Christine, who put almost every waking minute into concentrating on her role.

Charles would tease her about being a work-a-Hollywood-ic. "Ease up. 24/7 is a bit much."

"Charlie, nothing will ever take me away from our special time together. You are the love of my life. I know I'm engrossed in this role—my first—and I want to give it my best effort. But you are always on my mind and in my heart."

"Chris, I want you to have the success you dreamed of. I'll always be there for you."

*   *   *

About halfway through filming, there was another incident on the set. While Christine was resting on a captain's chair between scenes, she suddenly heard a whisper behind her. "Hey, Baby. Looking good."

She recognized the voice and whirled around to face Blake. "Get away from me, you jerk. Haven't you made enough trouble?"

"Only trying to be friendly. When you get tired of your boyfriend, I'll be there to catch you on the rebound."

"Don't hold your breath. Get away from me."

"Come on, don't be difficult. We hit it off before . . ."

Suddenly, a loud shout interrupted him. "Blake, get the hell away from her." Charles was approaching them. "I told you if you ever bothered her again, you'd be sorry." With that, Charles hauled off and landed a solid blow to Blake's face.

Christine got hysterical, crying out for help. At this point, the two men were at it with a vengeance. Members of the crew broke up the fight. Blake was bleeding and issuing threats as they carried him off the set. Charles had a cut on his face and was slightly disheveled.

Mr. V., who had missed the fracas, came rushing over to Charles. "What the hell is going on here?"

When Charles told him about Blake, Mr. V. asked, "Isn't he the one you believe trashed Christine's trailer?"

"Yes."

"Well, he's got to go. He's history on this set. I'll see to it that he never gets any work around here. Charles, do you want to press charges against him? That's what he deserves."

"I'll handle it my way, Mr. V. Thanks. He'll get what he deserves."

After a brief respite, they resumed shooting. However, the intensity of the situation was not lost on anyone. Many felt it was bad luck because a tension had been created that might affect the completion of the film. Mr. V. spoke reassuringly to the cast and crew, called for a coffee break, and invited Charles and Christine to join him.

"I hope you won't do anything foolish, Charles. Scum like that doesn't deserve anyone's attention. He belongs in jail, but how can we get the evidence? He's a slick one. Does things just short of an arrest. I don't want anything bad to happen to you kids, and not just because of the movie. I'm fond of both of you."

"Thanks, Mr. V. Don't worry about us. We'll be on our toes. He's not going to spoil anything. I'll see to that."

"Again, please do not do anything foolish."

"It won't be foolish."

Mr. V. and Christine exchanged glances. An unspoken concern lay between them.

*   *   *

The director was as good as his word. The following morning, before he scheduled shooting, he called Blake aside and berated him for his unacceptable behavior.

Blake started to stammer, apologizing, "I'm truly sorry, Mr. Victor, I meant no harm, I . . ."

Mr. V. looked at him scornfully. "You are fired. And don't think the business of the trailer is over yet. If I can help it, you will never work in this industry again."

Blake protested. "You've got to believe me. I had nothing to do with it."

"I believe Ms. O'Hara. Why would I take the word of someone like you? Apparently, your reputation leaves much to be desired."

The color in Blake's cheeks turned a rosy hue. The sharp edge to his voice was not lost on the director as he retaliated. "It's not wise to listen to lies and lies are exactly what your prima donna and her boyfriend are telling. I . . ."

"Mr. Dugan, I have no desire to continue this conversation. Get off the set at once, before the cast arrives. At least, save yourself that embarrassment."

Blake hesitated. He looked as though he had more to say, then turned abruptly toward the door.

Mr. V. watched him and thought, I've directed a lot of exits but this one is the best yet.

Within the half-hour, the cast and crew began arriving. When the announcement was made that Blake had been fired, a hush was followed by enthusiastic applause.

Shooting progressed without incident much to the joy of the unit production manager. Time limits and coverage of the script pages were well within financial estimates, in spite of the day lost when Christine's trailer was messed up.

A cameraman is an actor's best friend, especially when the camera loves its subject; and in this case, the camera and the cameraman loved Christine. Her lovely, refined features photographed to perfection, especially with Charles providing every advantage. He was excellent at his trade, using his camera as an artist, his brushes. The result was a stunning Christine.

The dailies were a testament to a fine collaboration. Everyone had positive expectations. The consensus was that the film would be a mega-box office block buster.

With only a few weeks of shooting left, Christine and Charles began making plans to live together. They could now afford to give up both apartments and find a more suitable place in Beverly Hills. Their realtor found exactly what they were looking for and a deal was made.

"Oh, Charlie, I can't ask for anything more. It's all so perfect." A tear fell to either side of her nose. Charles gently wiped them away with his handkerchief.

"You deserve it, Christine. What say we go to the Pub for old times' sake and celebrate.?"

"You betcha!"

"Now, now, young lady," Charles said with mock sarcasm, "you've got to lose that déclassé expression. In Hollywood, it's all about image."

"It's lost . . . you betcha."

Charles had to laugh. "You're adorable when you're naughty."

At the Pub, they decided to have supper so they slipped into a small booth to the rear of the bar. Although the menu was sparse, it was good. Irish Stew was a favorite so Charles ordered it for both of them, with "two Cosmopolitans, please".

When the waitress returned with their food, a sudden commotion started across the room. The barkeep, Tim, was yelling. "You get out of here and never come back or I'll turn you in."

An unmistakable, familiar voice retorted, "Why don't you mind your own business and stay behind the bar where you belong?"

Christine and Charles exchanged glances. It was Blake.

"Let's leave, Charlie."

"Stay put, Honey. I don't want him to see us."

The bartender came around from behind the bar and was forcefully ushering Blake out the front door. "I don't want to see your miserable face ever again, you low-life."

There was a mumbled threat as the door slammed.

Charles walked over to speak with Tim. "What was that all about?"

"That no good pusher was trying to sell cocaine to my customers. This isn't the first time. I suppose I should have called the police on him before, but I felt sorry for him—you know, down and out actor . . ."

"He's one dude you shouldn't waste your pity on. I know the guy. He deserves everything he gets."

"Well, I hope that's the last of him. The Pub as always been a favorite place for neighborhood people, famous or otherwise."

"Do me a favor, Tim. Keep an eye and ear open. Maybe you can learn some more about this guy. I'd be interested. I'll drop in again, alone."

"Will do, Mr. Markham. Always liked you and Ms. O'Hara. You're good people."

Charles returned to the booth and ordered nightcaps. They tried hard to pick up the remnants of what had begun as an enjoyable evening. Charles could not hide his irritation. "That s.o.b. is like a disease. It's time to find a cure."

"Charlie, please, you're frightening me."

He kissed her on the cheek and sipped his drink slowly. Enough is enough.

*   *   *

When Blake bolted from the Pub, he headed for LaBrea Street where he had some 'connections'. He also had some explaining to do to one of them. Too bad that bartender got on his case. There had been some good hits there. Well, he thought, I'll go back later, at closing time, and maybe catch a few buyers on the sidewalk. Too bad that bitch had complained to the escort service about him. It was nice money, but this was even better, if he could make the right contacts. His mind jumped from one idea to another then he saw Tony and Bill and greeted them. "How's it going, guys?"

Bill answered, "Cool. But you better watch it. Iggy's been looking for you . . . looking real mean."

"Yeah. Well, I've gotta talk to him. Ran into a little trouble."

"You'd better come up with something. Iggy gets off on hurting people real bad."

"Bull. He doesn't scare me." Blake smirked.

"Oh, no? Who does scare you, you weasel?" Iggy appeared suddenly, his face a threatening mask.

Blake stood frozen. His voice quavered as he tried to explain. "Just kidding. I didn't mean anything. It was only a joke."

"Well, let's see how funny this is." He jammed a pistol under Blake's jaw and cocked the hammer.

"Please, Iggy, I'll get the money soon, I swear. I've got this guy that owes me . . ." He felt his pants get wet as urine ran down his legs.

His fear was not lost on Iggy, who was in no mood to spend more time with Blake. He had a date with a girl who was really hot and he was anxious to get to her. In an unusual, benevolent mood, he told Blake, "You're a lucky man tonight. I'll give you until ten p.m. Friday night, right here. Pull any funny stuff and you're done. Understand?"

"Yes, Iggy, thanks. Ten o'clock. Friday. I'll be here with the money, I swear." His whole body shook as he watched the dealer disappear down the street. How the hell can I make this happen in five days? He turned slowly, waving a hand at Bill and Tony.

Better get home and put on some dry pants.

CHAPTER EIGHT

In a business where everything operates point by point, every step by a separate consideration, Blake Dugan had not had the slightest idea of how drug operations functioned. The only thing he had known was how to get a fix now and then.

That's where Bill and Tony had entered the picture. At first, Blake regarded them as a couple of out-of-work habitués of LaBrea Street. Tony, the less attractive of the two, was short and stocky, with thinning black hair. His eyes shifted from side to side like a frightened animal. Bill, on the other hand, was tall and lanky, with good features and blond, sun-streaked hair. From the way he spoke, Blake estimated that he had some acting experience. He did most of the talking while Tony echoed an occasional "Yeah" or "Dat's right".

They hadn't spoken, at first, but after nodding to each other on occasion, Tony said, one night, "Hey, how're ya doin'?"

A surprised Blake answered, "Not bad. Glad we're finally getting to meet. Name's Blake." Street smart, he sensed they had similar interests.

Bill spoke up. "Noticed you connecting with a couple of guys on the street. What do you use?"

Blake decided not to hedge. "Why? Got anything worthwhile? I'm into cocaine myself. After all, what's a nose for if not to 'blow'?" He grinned.

"We've got everything worthwhile, as long as you have the cash," Bill answered.

"No problem there." Blake scrutinized them. They looked well dressed. Didn't look hungry. This might prove to be mutually advantageous.

Bill said, "Tomorrow night, $300 and we'll take good care of you."

"See you then." Blake walked away. This would put a dent in his cash flow, but what the hell!

*   *   *

Blake had waited the following night and almost gave up on seeing them when they suddenly appeared and sidled over to him.

"Sorry to hang you up. Got some good stuff for you. Got the cash?" Bill asked.

"Sure." Blake took the money out of his wallet. "Can I get a whiff first?"

Tony stuck a small, plastic bag under his nose. "Breathe easy, this is the real McCoy."

The exchange was made and Blake hurried away.

Over the next few months, this transaction was repeated several times until Blake confessed that he was hard pressed financially and could no longer afford his habit. "Guess it's time to get a job. I'm not getting much in the movie industry, so I'm open to suggestions." Inwardly, he was hoping they'd give him a lead.

"Well," bragged Tony, "seein' as how we're connected, maybe we can do something . . ." A scathing look from Bill stopped him cold.

"Blake, let me talk to someone who might help you out, that is, if you are interested in the work . . ."

"Why don't I set up a meeting with a friend. If he likes you, he may have something for you."

"What kind of work? Not that I'm too particular . . ."

Blake was enthusiastic. "Great. I need something to fill the coffers until I get a casting call . . . if that ever happens."

Bill said, "If Iggy likes you, you won't have to worry about casting calls."

Tony's round, fleshy face lit up. "Ya gonna like Iggy."

Blake's brow furrowed. "What kind of a name is that? It's a kid's name."

Bill smirked. "Believe me, Iggy's no kid. You'll find that out soon enough. Be here tomorrow night about midnight. If you pass the test . . ."

"I'll be here. What do you mean by pass the test?"

"Better have all the right answers, my friend." Bill signaled Tony and they took off, leaving Blake to wonder what he had gotten himself into. Well, he thought, if it's dealing, I can handle that. If I can use the stuff, I can sell the stuff.

The next night, a well-groomed, nattily dressed man approached Blake, who couldn't help but notice the diamond pinky ring and the Rolex when the man extended his hand. "Blake Dugan?"

"Yessir, that's me."

"I heard from Bill and Tony you're looking for work. They tell me you're an all-right guy. You look like you've been around so there's no need for me to hedge." He then told Blake about the deal. He would be expected to move a certain amount of the product. "I'm looking to expand beyond LaBrea and I figure you, an actor, should have some interesting contacts."

"Yes, I know a lot of people."

"So, you're sure about getting enough action?"

"Absolutely, not to worry." Typical Blake. Always self-confident.

"That's what I'm counting on." Iggy handed Blake a piece of paper with the address of an old warehouse downtown. "Meet me there tomorrow afternoon. One o'clock and we'll talk. Just remember, what happens between us stays between us. Wouldn't want anything to go wrong." His eyes narrowed as he measured Blake.

"See you tomorrow. Don't worry. I know how to keep my mouth shut."

"I'm banking on it."

*   *   *

Now, several months later, Blake found himself facing a Friday night deadline with Iggy. He was stupid to have trusted that last buyer, a kid at the Pub and, worse, he got thrown out before he could collect. Now, he was in the hole for two grand. Well, it's not worth putting your life in jeopardy, he told himself. Just give Iggy the money from your stash.

Friday, he met Iggy and handed him the money. "See. I wouldn't let you down."

Iggy, with his arm around Blake's shoulders, complimented him for "coming through". "It's okay. Everybody makes mistakes sometime. Just don't let it happen again. I got big plans for you, my boy. Be patient."

As long as the plans were not at the end of a gun, Blake thought.

CHAPTER NINE

Since the episode at the Irish Pub, Christine and Charles chose to low key it for a while and spent most evenings at home, considering their heavy schedule. THE FLAWLESS MISTRESS was now in its final weeks of shooting the interior scenes. For the most part, schedules were being maintained and Mr. V. and the studio were satisfied with the progress. The cast had jelled well, especially Russ Crowell and Christine. They had a natural delivery that brought the needed reality to the film.

When he watched the rushes, Mr. V. exclaimed, "Audiences will love it. We have a hit on our hands. My stars are two of the most beautiful people in the cinema—and their talent—do I have to say more?"

Christine would blush with pleasure, and Russ, a smile playing around his lips, would wink at her. He would then pat Mr. V. on the back. "Happy to do it, Sir. But, we couldn't do it without you."

The director would beam at both of them and swallow hard.

* * *

Meanwhile, in the nefarious world in which Blake had taken domicile, he ingratiated himself with Iggy, so much so, that he now enjoyed Iggy's confidence. Blake had steadfastly made it a point to keep all his accounts on the straight and narrow, never missing a payoff to Iggy.

The money was good and Blake was now living large. He moved to an apartment in Hollywood Hills and had a wardrobe far better than any in his life. A couple of deals that were big, raised the ante and Blake now felt he had the world in the palm of his hand.

His thoughts often strayed to Christine but he decided to err on the side of caution and keep his distance until the time was right. Meanwhile, there were lots of twists and turns to navigate.

*   *   *

The advance publicity for THE FLAWLESS MISTRESS brought tremendous attention to the film and its stars. Their publicists arranged for every possible kind of public appearance. Adoring fans mobbed the sidewalks, begging for autographs which Christine and Russ graciously gave.

"Oh, Charlie, I feel like I'm in a dream. It's all so surreal."

"Enjoy the dream, my darling. You've earned it. Everyone loves you—but not as much as I do."

"It's all so perfect, sometimes it frightens me. Makes me wonder what's lurking in the wings."

Charles knew she was still fearful of Blake resurfacing, even though they hadn't seen or heard from him in months. "Christine, be happy. There's nothing to be concerned about except your career . . . and, of course, me." He smiled at her.

"You're right. I'm being foolish. Everything's so wonderful. I can't believe my good fortune."

"How about dinner at Chasen's tonight? We haven't been out on our own for a while."

"Great. I'll hop into a shower . . ."

He reached for her. "How about we both hop into a shower? I don't mind a late supper, if you don't," he teased.

"I do believe I would enjoy that."

Clothes went flying.

They arrived at Chasen's about ten p.m. The place was filled with people; members of the movie community and gawking tourists filled the room with conversation and laughter. When Christine and Charles entered the dining room, there was a flurry of excitement as patrons recognized her.

The maitre d' was gushing over them and immediately seated them at a prominent table. It was good for business. They ordered drinks from a more than willing waiter who fawned over them to a fault. Some movie folk stopped by to say Hello on their way out. Christine was amazed by the whole scene.

Charles said, "Baby, you've got to get used to this. This is for real and how it works."

"I know, Charlie, I'm getting there. It might help if you would pinch me once in awhile to show me I'm not dreaming."

The waiter returned with the menus and handed each one with an exaggerated flourish. Charles thought, Oh, no, not another wannabe. But, why not? Isn't everyone in Hollywood?

Supper was delicious, as usual. Chasen's was one of the oldest and most popular spots in town. "Nightcap, Chris?"

"Yes, please. Galliano with a wedge of lime, on the rocks, would be fine."

He ordered the drink and a Drambuie on the rocks for himself. As they sipped their drinks and whispered to each other, they became aware of someone nearby speaking in a loud voice, a familiar voice. Charles took Christine's hand in his and cautioned her not to turn around. When Charles lifted his head, he looked straight into the eyes of a well groomed, expensively dressed Blake Dugan.

"Well, if it isn't Hollywood's newest star," Blake said, coming over to the table.

Charles bolted up. "Get the hell away from here."

The maitre d' rushed toward them. "A problem? What is it?"

Charles said, "Get him out of here. He is upsetting Miss O'Hara."

Blake laughed. He turned to the maitre d'. Don't worry, Henri, I'm leaving. I just wanted to offer my best wishes."

Taking a step forward, Charles warned, "Get out right now or I'll handle this myself."

"I don't think you can, but . . . au revoir," Blake responded sarcastically.

Charles exercised control as he looked at Christine's pale face. Damn! They hadn't spoken about him for months; now he turns up just as repulsive as ever, looking like he won the lottery. Wonder what he's up to? I'm going to nail that creep, if it's the last thing I do.

They finished their drinks. Henri couldn't stop apologizing for "zat terrible man" as he escorted them across the room. There was a bit of a buzz in the restaurant as Charles quickly ushered Christine out to their waiting car.

*   *   *

At home, nothing was said. Neither of them wanted to bring up the incident. "How about watching an old movie?" Charles suggested. "I don't think I'm ready to go to sleep just yet. How about you?"

"Good idea, Charlie. I'm wide awake."

Ironically, the late movie was CAPE FEAR, a thriller about a stalker. They switched to a talk show instead. Finding little interest in the trite reportage and obvious attempts at humor, Christine and Charles soon fell sound asleep, snuggled in each other's arms on the couch.

When they awoke suddenly, sunlight was streaking through the huge living room windows. A slight noise at the door drew their attention. A key was turning in the lock and within seconds the housekeeper was standing in the doorway.

Christine sighed with relief. "Oh, thank God it's you, Bonita."

"What's wrong, Senora? I didn't mean to scare you."

"Oh, no, nothing . . . everything's all right. We just fell asleep out here"

"I'll start in the kitchen, okay?"

"Yes, yes, of course. Thank you. We have to get ready."

Christine and Charles showered and dressed quickly. They would just make it on time to the set. He could tell by her behavior that she still felt uneasy. Wish she'd get over the nervousness, he thought. But, then again, who could blame her?

They arrived on set, on time. Mr. V. had an ambitious schedule for the day. "Come, come, darlings, take your places. We have a lot to do." In an instant, cameramen and crew stood ready as the actors took their places for the scene.

Charles noticed, with pride, that Christine was immediately in character and delivered her lines with confidence. Working with an established star such as Russ Crowell provided the necessary added inspiration.

After the day's shooting, Mr. V. called the cast and crew together. "I have news. We may be filming the vacation scenes on location. Maybe Mexico or South America. Maybe the Riviera. I'm not sure. Meanwhile, have your passports ready."

"How exciting!" Christine hugged Charles. "Just think, we'll get away from here for awhile. Charlie I'm so looking forward to a change of scene. It'll be good for us."

*   *   *

After Blake's rebuff at Chasen's, he was more determined than ever to spoil things for Christine and Charles. He was consumed with jealousy and a desire for vengeance. However, he had to put that on hold. His dealings with Iggy had earned him a lot of money. As time went on, Iggy increasingly trusted Blake. One night, on LaBrea, he said, "Ya know Blake, I'm thinking, you might step up in the chain. You've been doing good. You've got a classy look and you know how to talk right. How'd you feel about traveling?"

"What do you have in mind?"

"I'm willing to move you up, if you think you can handle it. I'd like you to be a runner for me . . . what we call a 'mule'. You'll be dealing directly with one of the cartels. I know you like money and mules get paid real good. Ready for this?"

Blake had heard stories about shootouts and bodies dumped after deals gone wrong; but he also heard of successful runs and big payoffs. "Sure, Iggy. I think I can handle it. What's the scoop?"

The two men talked for hours. Iggy laid out a plan wherein Blake would do business directly with a drug baron in a town near the Mexican border. This contact was a source for marijuana and cocaine. "And, don't worry, the right people have been paid to look the other way. The Baron will provide safe escort across the border. He's been drug trafficking for years, with no problems."

"Hard to believe all this going on—with aliens sneaking into the U. S. Seems like they're watching closely, but they keep getting in . . . and so do the drugs."

"We got it all figured out. There's a lot of commercial traffic going to and from Mexico—produce, building materials, clothing—we're connected."

Blake, shrugged. "Well, okay then, I'm in."

"Good boy. Meet me at the warehouse next Tuesday, seven p.m. I'll have the whole thing set up for you. Get ready for a little excitement and mucho money."

"Sounds good. I'm ready."

In spite of all his bravado, Blake wondered what he was getting into. In this dark world of drug dealing, he had seen the struggling, the denial, and even the death of users. His conscience never bothered him because he believed that people made their choices and deserved to live—or die—with them. Right now, his choice was to make a lot of money to have the life he visualized for himself. Everything—*everyone*—will fall into place, he assured himself.

CHAPTER TEN

It had been quite a while since Charles had spent any time with Jim; however, they did keep in touch by phone. Each promised the other that they would get together soon, but somehow, it didn't happen. Finally, after leaving the set one day, Charles asked Christine, "Honey, I've really been neglecting Jim. Would you mind if we got together some night?"

"Of course not. I'm usually pooped after a day's shoot. Call Jim and have a boys' night out. You've earned it."

Charles immediately called Jim. "How about tomorrow night, just the two of us. We've got a lot of catching up to do. Irish Pub, at seven?"

Charles suggested the Pub because he wanted to get some input from Tim, the bartender, about Blake. The night he and Christine stopped in for a drink, Tim had thrown Blake out because he was dealing drugs. Meeting Jim there would serve a dual purpose.

When Charles arrived, Jim was already at the bar, beer in hand. The two men exchanged warm greetings.

"Being in love must agree with you, Charlie. You look wonderful."

"Jim, I can't tell you how much it agrees with me. Christine is just an amazing woman. She's got beauty, talent . . ."

Jim cut in. "Okay, okay. I think I noticed all that before you did. Remember? You didn't even want to invite her for a drink. Good thing you listened to old Jimbo."

"You got that right."

"So, tell me everything. How's the new house and living together? What movie are you working on now?"

"Everything is just super; the house is lovely, we're happy, and the movie is THE FLAWLESS MISTRESS. We still have a couple of weeks of shooting left. However, there's still one flaw in the ointment."

"I thought so. You can't fool me, my friend. I could tell by the strained sound of your voice that something was bothering you. I'm afraid to ask, but I will. Is that scoundrel Blake still lurking in the shadows?"

"Hit the nail on the head. He's no longer in the shadows. I've come close to decking him. But, let me tell you what happened one night when Christine and I stopped here for a drink." He then went on to describe the incident.

"Can't you nail the s.o.b.? That would put him away for a long time."

"You don't know how many times I wanted to have him arrested, but Christine goes bonkers. She doesn't want to be involved with him in any way, even an arrest, and surely not now when she is starring in her first film. I don't want to upset her."

Tim came over to pour another drink. Charles asked, "Any news on that character, Blake—the one you threw out of here?"

"No sir, Mr. Markham. Haven't seen hide nor hair of him. I did hear though that he connected with a couple of guys on LaBrea and does his business elsewhere, if you know what I mean. He's bad news."

"Thanks, Tim." Charles turned to Jim. "Well, I guess Blake's found his niche. No wonder he looked prosperous. There must be a way to put that guy behind bars."

"Charles, I've got an assignment coming up on the ills and evils of Sunset Strip. Maybe your boy is working that area."

"Jim, you can't imagine how much I would appreciate any info you can find on this creep. Seeing him put away will be my biggest pleasure."

"I'll be on it. Don't worry. Now, let's relax and talk about something pleasant."

The two men reminisced about the bachelor evenings they spent in Charles' old apartment . . . something they both missed . . . but Jim admitted that Charles had lucked out big time. "I'm happy for you," Jim said, with sincerity.

"Thanks. I hope you and I never lose touch. You're a good friend, Jim."

They parted company early. Charles had to be on the set at eight a.m. and Jim had to report for assignment at eight, as well.

"Will be in touch," Jim promised.

*   *   *

When Charles arrived at his house, he entered quietly because he expected Christine to be sound asleep. To his surprise, she came running out of their bedroom, into his arms. "Oh, Charlie, I'm so glad you're home. I couldn't sleep. My imagination got the best of me, I guess. I kept thinking I heard movements outside but there was no one there when I turned on the flood lights. Guess I only feel secure when you're with me."

"Not to worry, Chris. I'm here and you're safe in my arms. Now to sleep, to dream . . ."

She hugged him. "I love it when you go poetic on me. Goodnight, Darling."

Down the road, in the dark, Blake muttered to himself, "Boy, that was close." Charles had come home sooner than he expected. He was crouching just below their bedroom window when he heard the car pull in. The only escape route was through the huge ficus hedge surrounding the property. As he forced his way through the sturdy branches, he could feel the scratches on his face and fingers. The wear and tear on his expensive suit was not lost on him, either. Damn! Who would have thought Charles would be home so early. It was only by luck that Blake had seen him sitting at the Pub bar when he passed by.

Now, as he raced down the quiet, dark street to his car and drove away, all he could think of was how close he had come.

Well, time was on his side and there was lots of money yet to be made. Iggy told him that he would be meeting with the drug baron in Mexico within the next few days. What a trip that'll be—in more ways than one.

Blake returned to his apartment, showered and doctored his wounds. The night was still young so he dressed in a pure silk, blue shirt and expensive navy slacks. A pair of designer loafers completed the look he wanted. He headed for the Hyatt Regency for a nightcap and . . . you never know.

*   *   *

The loud, jangling of the phone startled Blake. He had just fallen asleep after an enjoyable late night with a pick up. "Hello, who's this?"

"Blake, it's Iggy. Meet me this afternoon, three o'clock, at the warehouse." The phone went dead before Blake could respond.

Must be about the new route, he figured. "I'm ready for the big time," he said to no one in particular. Three o'clock can't come fast enough. A few hours of sleep and I'm off to bigger and better things.

He dozed off into a deep sleep and awoke, suddenly, with a start. What time was it? The clock read a few minutes after two in the afternoon. I'd better get my ass in gear if I'm going to make it by three. Iggy did not like to be kept waiting.

Blake's car screeched to a halt in front of the building at a minute of three. He hurried inside and up the stairs, across the landing to the office in the back. Iggy was there, smoking up a storm, as usual. His standard bottle of scotch was open on the table and a half-filled glass was in his hand. "Well, Romeo, had a busy night, did we? I'd just about given up on you."

"Don't worry about me. I'll always show." He shifted his feet from side to side.

Blake's nervousness was obvious to Iggy. "I hope so. I got a lot goin' on you." He narrowed his eyes for a moment and then laughed loudly. "Come on, my boy. Sit down. Have a drink; let's talk."

"I'm all ears," a calmer Blake answered.

"Good." Iggy paused. "Remember my telling you I was going to hook you up with one of the drug barons in Mexico? Everything is in place for a new mule—that'll be you—and the Baron is looking forward to your first run. Ready?"

"Right on."

"Ojinaga is an important, secretive smuggling point on the United States-Mexican border. The town is located along the Rio Grande near Big Bend National Park. The Baron has access to the best marijuana and his cocaine comes from Columbia. His operation is smooth and without interference."

"How does he manage to remain untouched?"

Iggy looked hard at him. "That's something you don't have to worry about . . . unless you screw up. We take care of the right people. Follow?"

"Yeah, sure." Blake sensed Iggy's irritation. "No more questions."

"Good. Now, listen carefully. Tomorrow night at exactly midnight be here waiting at the side door. A large trailer truck marked 'Green Products' will pull up. Hop into the back of the truck which will be filled with crates of vegetables. You'll find a briefcase in back of the middle crate with a hundred grand in it. When you get to the meeting place in Mexico, there will be three men waiting for you. Your driver will ride shotgun, so you're covered. If they insist on you opening the case first, do it. Then, you tell them to show you the merchandise. It should be an easy exchange. You count the kilos; they count the money."

"When do I meet the main man?"

After the deal is made. Don't worry. Everything will fall into place. Just go with the flow."

Blake was almost at ease but as they were leaving, Iggy suddenly handed him a gun, saying, "Just in case."

"But, but . . ." Blake began to stammer.

Iggy strode rapidly away. "Good luck." The words floated back to Blake.

In his apartment, Blake paced up and down, considering the circumstances in which he found himself. He had gone beyond the pale with Iggy and now he'd better come through.

*   *   *

The midnight run to Mexico went smoothly. Blake easily found the briefcase in between the crates of vegetables. He spent the whole trip sitting in the passenger seat, trying to drum up conversation with Louie, the driver, who seemed intent on watching the road. The lack of communication frustrated Blake, who persisted in asking questions. "You been driving these runs long?"

"Yep."

"Ever have any trouble with the border patrol?"

"Nope." Louie sounded annoyed.

"Come on, fella, give me a break. What can I expect when we get to the border?"

Finally, an answer. "You just sit quietly. I'll handle it."

"Jesus, this is my first run. Give me a clue." Blake began to squirm.

"Listen, Buster, I'll call the shots when I need to. Meanwhile, keep your eyes and ears open and your mouth shut."

Blake thought it best not to show his irritation. This jerk's a big help. The last thing I need is to make a mistake.

A few hours later, they approached the border and he noticed that Louie opted for the furthest lane even though a closer one was available. Must be one of the cogs in the wheel. Louie extended a hand out his window. "*Como estas, amigo?* Nice to see you."

The border guard replied, "*Si,* and you, *Senor.* Now, *por favor,* please open the back of the truck."

Blake felt perspiration trickle down his neck; his scalp felt damp. What the hell?

Louie turned to Blake. "Don't sweat it. Get out and open the back of the truck so the inspector can check the produce—and take this with you." He winked at Blake and smiled. "Make sure Geraldo get these 'papers' when he is **inside**." Louie handed him an envelope.

Blake watched as Geraldo played a large flashlight over the contents of the truck. "Everything looks fine, *amigo.*" Blake handed him the envelope and they shook hands. "It has been a pleasure. I look forward to seeing you again."

I'll bet you do, Blake mused. Never saw anyone so happy. Wonder how much the payoff is? Back in the passenger seat, he was tempted to ask Louie about it. Looking at his deadpan face, he decided not to.

They headed for the meeting place which turned out to be a deserted airplane hangar on the outskirts of Mexico City. Louie drove in and turned the truck around to face the huge, open hangar doors. He learned a long time ago to never get caught with his back to the door. After 15 minutes in silence, he said, "Okay, it's show time."

A black BMW suddenly appeared. Three men emerged. 'Hey, Louie, your cousin is here," one of them said.

"Yeah, which one?"

"Tomassino."

Louie turned to Blake. "It's okay. Pick up the briefcase and get out of the truck. Don't worry, I got your back."

The three men approached. The one carrying a large suitcase spoke up. "Open your briefcase, *Senor.*"

Blake obliged. He noticed a familiar bulge in the pockets of the other two. The one who had spoken checked the wrapped C notes. When he indicated that it was satisfactory, Blake said, "Now, please, show me the product."

They obliged and Blake counted the packaged kilos of cocaine. At random, he slit one open and made the test, as Iggy had instructed. There was no conversation during the exchange. Everything was in order.

As the BMW disappeared from view, another one appeared, pulling up alongside them. A tinted window slid down and the driver addressed Louie: "You will follow our car. It's not a long ride, as you well know."

Louie nodded. "Will do."

Go with the flow, Iggy had told Blake. He turned to Louie. "You're the driver."

It was early dawn when the two vehicles mounted a long, steep driveway at the head of which stood a palatial mansion. The lead vehicle continued on its way.

"Holy shit!" Blake muttered under his breath. "No wonder they call him the Baron."

"Hold your water. You ain't seen nuthin' yet."

"Okay, Jolson," Blake shot back. He got a blank look from Louie.

They were greeted at the door by a butler who ushered them into a tastefully furnished expansive living room that opened out to a huge patio facing an enormous lake. Blake looked around. There was no shortage of bodyguards. The place was swarming with them. Firearms were visible and in abundance; surveillance cameras, strategically placed. Boy, try to get out of here untouched if you rub someone the wrong way.

A maid came in carrying trays of food and hot coffee. The butler stood ready to pour drinks. "The Baron will join you in a moment. Please make yourselves comfortable."

Blake and Louie were tired but they were hungry and thirsty, as well, so they were quick to pick up on the butler's invitation.

"Good morning, gentlemen." A tall, well-tanned, mustachioed man, with a mane of black hair to his shoulders, greeted them. His looks and his accent defined his ethnicity. The Baron was dressed in black leather trousers, custom designed silk shirt, and a satin, embossed smoking jacket. His boots were of the finest leather and shone with a high luster.

Blake couldn't help thinking: perfect casting. After all the riff-raff he had dealt with on the Strip, he marveled at the elegance of the Baron and his surroundings. Wow, he thought. I'm working at the wrong end of this business.

Conversation with the Baron consisted mainly of questions posed to Blake. The Baron was interested. "You impress me as a clever fellow . . . someone who can handle himself well under any conditions. I hope to see more of you, Senor Blake."

Louie squelched an impulse to laugh. He couldn't help but think what impression the Baron would have had if he heard their conversation in the truck on the way down.

CHAPTER ELEVEN

The word back on LaBrea was that Iggy's mule was right on the money. Blake had made several successful runs and enjoyed a generous share of the profits, plus a bonus—some of the finest coke in town.

Iggy told Blake about a transaction he would be handling directly with the Baron.

"You'll be carrying a mil." Iggy said

"That is big."

"The Baron likes your style." Iggy patted Blake on the back.

"And I like his."

"Who wouldn't? That's living more than large, that's living huge—but dangerous," Iggy said. "Always has to watch his back. Other cartels are always trying to take over and, believe me, it gets pretty bloody out there."

Blake felt uneasy. He didn't enjoy hearing about that side of the business.

"Yeah," Iggy continued, "if you want to get rid of somebody, it's off with his head."

Blake looked at Iggy in disbelief. "You kidding me? I thought that only happened in the Middle East."

Iggy laughed. "Sure. Anyway, not to worry. The Baron has things under control."

Even though Blake had heard about drug wars, it never occurred to him that he would ever be involved. This is one part I don't want to play. I hope my ass is covered.

*   *   *

While Blake was making his mark in the underworld of drugs, Christine was busy filming THE FLAWLESS MISTRESS. After the indoor stage scenes were a wrap, the director advised the cast and crew, "We are going on location to Mexico City for the final scenes of the film. Plan on leaving within seventy-two hours." He cautioned against inviting any PR. "The paparazzi will hound us and disrupt the shooting schedule. So, please, everyone—a tight lid on this. Thanks."

*   *   *

Charles was in constant touch with Jim, who was still working on his "Ills and Evils of Sunset Strip" assignment. He'd been gathering material by ingratiating himself with some shady characters on the street.

One night, he heard some talk from two fellows with whom he had become friendly: Bill and Tony. Bill was kind of tight lipped but Tony had a loose tongue, and always put his foot in his mouth. "Ya know, we're connected guys." He loved to brag. "We set up one of our friends and he made it big."

Remembering what Charles told him about Blake's appearance, Jim took a shot. "Yeah, I heard about that guy—good looking actor type—Blake something?"

Big mouth blurted out, "Yeah, that's him."

Bill scowled. "We don't really know him or if that's even his name. Right Tony?"

Tony got the message. "Yeah. That's right."

Jim hoped that he didn't show how welcome the news was. He changed the subject. "What do you say, we grab a cup of coffee at the diner? It's getting a little chilly. My treat."

As they sipped coffee and munched doughnuts, Jim kept the conversation light. There was no further reference to anyone named Blake.

Back at his apartment, Jim gave himself a thumb's up, followed by a loud "Yes!"

The next morning, he called Charles. "I think I'm onto something." He recounted the conversation with Tony and Bill.

"That's great, Jim. But be careful. I wouldn't want you to have any trouble over this. That's a dangerous bunch down there."

"Listen, my friend, you know how diplomatic I can be. These guys like me. They consider me a good customer." He couldn't help laughing. "I never cared for the stuff and I get rid of it as soon as I get back to the apartment. Anything for a good story—and you might get rid of that thorn in your side."

"Jim, Mr. V. told us that we are going to Mexico City, on location. He believes he can finish shooting within a month, as long as the weather holds out. Meanwhile, we've got a hiatus. Christine and I will be tourists in Mexico City for a few days."

"Good. You deserve some fun. I'll call your cell phone only if I need to. Enjoy."

Jim felt a satisfaction in the progress he was making, not only with his story but because he was helping his friends. He sat down to type up his notes and then relaxed in front of the television, cold beer in hand. Tonight, he thought, I'll breeze over to the Strip and make some more small talk with Bill and Tony. I've only scratched the surface. My money is on big mouth. If only I could get Bill to open up more.

The Strip seemed unusually quiet. A few people were lingering around doorways and lamp posts. Something must be going down. Jim walked over to LaBrea and caught up with Bill and Tony who seemed nervous.

"What's happening, fellows?' Jim asked. "Seems really quiet tonight."

"Yeah," Tony answered. "Big bust on the Strip. Cops hauled in a couple of the working girls and boys—caught one of the gang pushers right in the middle of a deal."

Bill was not too talkative. "Just playing it safe. Keeping a low profile. We beat it when the police were making the bust."

"Smart move," Jim agreed. He waited a couple of seconds. No further conversation was forthcoming. He began to feel awkward standing there. The boys were playing it cagey.

Suddenly, Bill spoke up. "It's strange how the cops made a move tonight. We were wondering if it was spur of the moment or they knew something was going down." He jerked his head back and stared at Jim.

"Hey, guys, you know how things work," Jim said. "The police make these sudden raids hoping to catch a deal in progress—once in a while they get lucky."

"You might be right," Bill replied.

They made small talk for a while, then Jim said, "Think I'll turn in early tonight. Need something to relax me."

"We can help you with that." Bill carefully reached into his pants' pocket. He looked around cautiously before he slipped a small plastic bag into Jim's hand. "Just enough to make life pleasant, eh?" A crooked smile displayed bad teeth in an otherwise handsome face.

Jim palmed Bill several hundred dollar bills. He had done this before many times in order to establish a relationship with "the boys", as he referred to them. Their cue was "need something to relax me" and coke and money exchanged hands.

The three of them stood quietly for a few minutes, their eyes searching the dimly lit street to make sure there was no one around that could spell trouble.

Jim said his goodnight and headed for home.

Bill and Tony disappeared into the darkness.

Jim realized how much he was depending on their information. It had taken careful maneuvering to convince them of his friendship. Time was running out; his editor was pushing him hard.

When he got back to his apartment, he flushed the packet of white powder down the toilet. Thank goodness for his expense account. He took a cold beer out of the fridge, plunked down on the couch and wondered what his next move should be. Tomorrow morning he would check the police docket. Maybe he could find something interesting on the bust that went down that night.

After a few hours, he fell asleep on the couch. In his dreams, he was still on LaBrea doing deals with Bill and Tony and being chased by the cops. He awoke with a start at three in the morning. "Guess it's time to go to bed." He laughed as he yawned and rubbed his head. "That's one dream I hope never comes true," he said to himself as he washed his face and brushed his teeth vigorously. He hopped into bed. Tossing and turning, he finally gave up and headed for another beer. Dawn came quickly.

CHAPTER TWELVE

There was much excitement and preparation going on at the Paramount lot. Props and flats were being readied for transport to Mexico City. Location shots for THE FLAWLESS MISTRESS required special effects because the film was a period piece. Indoor and outdoor scenes had to be "aged" accordingly. A multitude of racks stood waiting for the costumes they would carry. Mr. V., always totally immersed in every aspect of his film, raced around yelling instructions to the movers. The trucks would travel by night to avoid daytime congestion on the highways. The E.T.A. for Mexico City was early the next morning.

Charles and Christine busied themselves packing and shutting down the house. Their friends next door had volunteered to keep tabs on things during their absence.

"Charlie, I can hardly wait to get there. I've never been out of the States before. Mexico City sounds like such a fabulous place. I've been looking at brochures . . ."

"Sweetheart, don't get overly impressed by them. They only show the glitz and the glamour. I've been to Mexico . . . not always the safest place . . . but it is colorful. It's Margarita country. That's fun."

"Charlie, when we finish filming we're going to a secluded villa on the water where we can swim nude and sun ourselves and just relax."

"I'm with you all the way. But right now we've got to finish packing. Pick up will be here shortly."

"What time is the limo coming for us?"

"About six o'clock. That'll get us to the hotel in time for a late supper."

"Charlie, do you think we can take in the city night lights? These few days will be our last chance to relax until the movie's a wrap."

"Sure, Baby." From what Charles had observed on previous trips to Mexico, extreme caution was always advised, especially at night . . . but why say more now to spoil Chris' expectations.

"Charlie, you're frowning."

"I didn't realize that I was. Guess I'm trying to digest too much at one time." He hugged her. "We're going to have the best time of our lives."

She laughed. "You betcha!"

He retaliated with a quick swat at her derriere.

*   *   *

Blake Dugan was riding high. The Baron enjoyed his company, so much so that soon all of Blake's deals were completed at the mansion. Even Iggy was amazed. Never before had the Baron operated this way with his mules. The people to whom Iggy answered were more than satisfied. Blake, being in the good graces of the Baron, assured them a "good place" for supplies, as long as the Baron survived the cartel wars . . . a constant threat.

One night, after the usual exchange of suitcases, the Baron sent Louie from the room. He turned to Blake. "Sit down, my boy. What would you think if I asked you to work for me? I need a good man in my organization—one I can trust to make major deals with important people." He lit one of his Cuban cigars, took a puff and exhaled as he studied Blake's reaction.

Staring in disbelief, Blake stammered, "Sir, I don't know what to say . . ."

"Say yes. You will represent me at special conferences in California with the highest level principals. I have been observing you carefully. You are one smart *hombre*. You handle yourself well and you look fine. Of course, it will mean that you will change your place of residence." He took another long drag on his cigar.

Blake flinched. A move like that might change his plans but, monetarily, it might expedite things. He didn't relish the idea of leaving L.A. but because he would be traveling back and forth to California, he could make it his business to be in L.A. when he had to. He smiled at the Baron. "Thank you for your offer. It will be an honor."

"You will tell no one of our arrangement. The competition is keen and dangerous."

"I know how to keep my mouth shut."

"Good!" The Baron extended his hand and they shook on it. "Done."

*   *   *

Blake and Louie returned to L.A. and met with Iggy at the warehouse where they delivered a suitcase filled with the finest cocaine from Columbia. They, in turn, received a case filled with American dollars, which they split between them. Louie took off immediately.

Blake hesitated. How in hell do I tell Iggy I'm leaving? I could get myself killed. "Iggy, I'm going to have to leave for awhile . . . got a gig in Mexico to do a movie."

"Whadyya mean, you're leaving? Why? You've done damn well with us."

"I know and I appreciate it but I couldn't turn down this offer. You know, I'm an actor first."

"I know you're a jerk," Iggy snapped. "We have big plans for you . . ."

"I'm sorry but I can't let this chance go by. I'll be back as soon as the film's done." Blake didn't know what to expect next. It was like Russian Roulette.

Iggy was muttering under his breath. Nobody just leaves . . . who knows if Blake can keep his mouth shut . . . now I have to break in another mule. Men have been killed for less. What if Blake talks to the wrong people? Dammit, he really liked Blake.

"Come on, Iggy, we're friends. I'll do right by you, I swear."

Iggy decided to roll with the dice. "Just don't screw up, if you know what I mean, and watch who you talk to and what you say. My neck is on the line and so is yours."

"Read you loud and clear. Don't worry. See you soon." He turned and walked rapidly toward the door. This was too easy, he thought.

Blake arranged for the movers to deliver everything to Mr. Sean Ferguson at an address specified by the Baron. Just a decoy. In actuality, he would be living at the Baron's mansion.

For sentimental reasons, Blake decided to go over to Hollywood Boulevard where some of his acquaintances lived. Sure enough, he ran into one of the extras he had worked with in THE FLAWLESS MISTRESS. "Hey, Mark, how are you? Movie finished yet?"

"No, but I opted out. They're going on location to Mexico City. I got another gig. How about you?"

"What a coincidence. I've got a part in a movie filming in Mexico. Starts in a week. Good luck, Mark. Gotta run."

Well, well, Blake mused . . . Christine in Mexico City.

The move to Mexico was easily accomplished and soon Blake was comfortably established at the mansion. In the interim, he had grown a long mustache and chin hair. The actor in him had inspired the change—might as well look the part.

The Baron voiced his approval. "Ah, Blake, I see you are looking more like one of us. I like it."

Blake acknowledged the comment with a smile. He asked, "Is it all right if I take some free time today to enjoy the sights like a *touristo*?"

"Of course, enjoy. You are not needed presently. I will let you know when."

Blake changed into casual clothes and took off for the City. He parked in a convenient spot near one of the busy restaurants. While he devoured a beef and cheese taco with a glass of beer, he casually asked the waitress, "What's happening around here? Anything interesting for a visitor like me? Is it true they are making a movie near the City?"

"*Si, Senor.* Everyone is so excited. It is always so when Hollywood comes here."

"Really. Where are they doing this?"

She explained that a huge part of an old estate had been rented by the movie company. "Many of us go to watch when we can."

"I would like to do that. Can you tell me how to get there?"

"Sure."

Blake followed her directions to the outskirts of the City. Eventually, he came upon the perimeter of the estate, obscured by thick underbrush and huge trees. He noticed that a small section had been worn down to a low fringe, obviously by the locals that gathered daily on the periphery to view the movie making. Blake joined them.

At that moment, Mr. V. was shooting a scene with Christine and Russ. When Blake saw her he swallowed hard. "God, she is more gorgeous than ever!" he exclaimed to no one in particular. As usual, his libido overrode whatever common sense he had. I'll risk anything to have her, he vowed.

A male extra had positioned himself several feet away to enjoy a cigarette. Blake recognized him at once. "Hey, Chuck, how's it going?"

The actor regarded him briefly. "Well, I'll be a . . . is that you, Blake? What are you doing in Mexico?"

"I'm here to work in a film. Top secret right now."

"Is that the reason for all the facial hair? Didn't recognize you, at first. Looks good."

"Thanks. So when does Mr. V. think he'll wind up?"

"Probably in a few weeks, if there are no hitches."

A few weeks, Blake thought. Not much time. I hope the Baron doesn't tie me up out of town for too long. Might have to alter my plan again. I can't afford to screw up.

He turned to Chuck. "Where are you guys holed up? Maybe we can have a drink some night."

"We're split up at a couple of hotels. Drink sounds good." He paused. "Hey, don't let Mr. V. see you. Remember . . ."

"Yeah, yeah, yeah. Big deal! He can't stop me from being here or anywhere, as long as I'm not on his damn set."

During this exchange, Blake's eyes blazed with anger. This was not lost on Chuck, who quickly put out his cigarette. "Well, good luck, break a leg and all that sort of stuff. Gotta get ready for the next scene." He bolted across the grass.

"You didn't tell me where you're staying," Blake yelled after him. To hell with him. Blake's eyes searched hungrily for the sight of Christine.

She was just finishing an emotional scene with Russ Crowell which ended in a deeply sensuous embrace and kiss.

Blake took a deep breath. Just wait, Beautiful.

*　　*　　*

When Blake returned to the mansion, the butler informed him that he was to be ready for dinner at eight o'clock. "The Baron is entertaining guests and he request a more formal attire than usual."

"Thanks." This news didn't please Blake. He had planned to make the rounds of some of the hotel bars in town hoping to run into cast members of THE FLAWLESS MISTRESS. Well, he thought, I'd better damn well dress for dinner . . . the choice is not mine. He showered, chose the appropriate clothing carefully, and at exactly eight o'clock, made his appearance. When he entered the dining room, all conversation came to a momentary halt. Blake was strikingly handsome in his striped navy blue suit, a crisp cotton lavender shirt and satin tie to match. Expensive black patent leather shoes completed the image. He was aware of the approval in the Baron's eyes as he introduced him.

After a splendid meal and typical dinner table conversation, the men retired to the library to enjoy Cuban cigars and nightcaps. The ladies went to the sitting room for their after dinner drinks and girl talk.

The Baron dragged on his cigar for a few moments then turned to Blake. "My friend, you and Eduardo are leaving for Columbia tomorrow morning."

So soon? Blake wondered. And, out of the country? He had other plans for the next day but he knew better than to resist. His soul was no longer his own—at least, not for a while. "Very well, Baron."

"Here is your passport and fake papers. You are now Sean Ferguson, Blake. Eduardo will accompany you. The flight is at eight o'clock in the morning. Once you arrive, Eduardo will take control. Just follow his instructions. You will be meeting with three contacts at a small airstrip near Medellin where you will exchange money for one thousand kilos of cocaine. The routine is standard. Count everything carefully and make the exchange. If all is well, a handshake and a speedy departure will follow. Everything is arranged for your quick return."

Blake had done the math mentally. This will bring a big payday—but what if the deal doesn't go down as planned? He swallowed hard—a reaction that was not lost on the Baron.

"Come, my friends, let us have one more drink and then join the ladies." The Baron puffed on his cigar, exhaling a cloud of unpleasant vapors. "I have a little entertainment planned for all of us." He glanced toward Blake. They needed to have a few minutes alone later. He didn't like what seemed a display of weakness. Then again, he reasoned, one could expect such a reaction from a novice. Anyway, the boy has potential.

Entertainment proved to be a sultry, attractive chanteuse who danced through a repertoire of sensuous songs of love and fiery songs of unrequited love and betrayal. Her audience sighed and applauded in the right places. All were enjoying themselves, especially the Baron who seemed taken with the dark beauty . . . but not so much that he didn't cast an occasional glance at Blake, who looked lost in thought. Had he overestimated the man?

By the time the evening ended, Blake's confidence had restored itself. He was relaxed and charming as could be. The Baron's guests gave him a nod of approval as each took his departure.

"You did well tonight, my boy. This is a tough crowd to please. They gave you the nod. Now, go to sleep and be ready early for your trip. Don't worry. No problem. Your first time out of the country, you can't help the butterflies. Just think of the benefits, eh?"

Blake smiled . . . the benefits, yeah. A lot of money and what it could bring him. "I'm fine. Nothing a good night's rest won't cure. I'll be ready to go on time."

"That's what I like to hear. Now, as I said, you and Eduardo will meet up with Carlos Modena at a small airstrip outside of Medellin. A driver will be waiting at the airport to take you there when you land. The chauffeur is a new man who will identify himself to Eduardo once he recognizes the insignia on the duffel bag you carry."

Blake was tempted to ask for more details but his trend of thought was interrupted.

"You have nothing to concern yourself with. Just follow Eduardo'a actions and learn."

Blake flashed a smile of self-assurance. Never let them see you sweat.

"Good night and good luck." The Baron walked away quickly.

Right then and there, Blake had more than his share of butterflies.

He was still awake when streams of early morning light filtered through his bedroom blinds. His brain felt muddled. Too many cigars. Too much booze. He yawned, stretched . . . his mouth tasted lousy. Blake bolted for the shower. Once washed and shaved, teeth brushed, he felt energized.

Dressed in casual clothes, he stood in the entrance hall at six a.m. The limo was already waiting outside. Eduardo appeared within minutes. "Ready?" He handed Blake a large, tan duffel bag that bore the trade mark of a popular women's wear.

"Lead on MacDuff," Blake said.

Eduardo glanced at him quizzically and shrugged. Crazy American.

Why would I think he'd recognize a line from Shakespeare, Blake thought, as he flashed Eduardo a friendly smile.

In the limo, the duffel bag sat on the seat between them. Within a short time, they arrived at the Mexico City International Airport, went through the usual, arranged check points and then boarded the plane to Columbia.

After they were comfortably set up in first class, Blake asked the hostess for a pillow. Maybe now he could catch some z's. Eduardo felt the same way. Soon, both men were sound asleep, the duffel bag tucked safely under their feet.

The stewardess shook them gently to tell them they would be landing shortly. "Is there anything I can get you? We land in Bogota in fifteen minutes."

CHAPTER THIRTEEN

The El Dorado International Airport in Bogota bustled with business people and tourists. Blake followed Eduardo to a huge waiting area where they were to meet their driver. Eduardo placed the duffel bag, with its insignia facing outward, in front of his feet.

Within a few seconds a chauffeur approached. "You are the gentlemen from La Signora Sportswear?"

"Si." Eduardo said.

"I have instructions to take you to your meeting. Follow me, please."

Eduardo put his arm out to stop Blake from moving. He turned to the chauffeur. "What is the name of the person who sent you?" Eduardo's right hand slipped inside his jacket and rested on the butt of the revolver tucked into his waistband. He stared at the chauffeur. "The name, *por favor.*"

The driver hesitated. Apparently, he hadn't expected resistance. "Perhaps I have made a mistake." He turned quickly and disappeared into the crowded airport.

Blake said, "I guess you can't be too careful."

Eduardo explained. That is an old cartel trick—trying to intercept a rival deal. You see, he didn't have the correct answer, so he ran like the slimy little lizard that he is."

Blake wanted to laugh but instead he took a deep breath. Good thing Eduardo called the shots correctly. This is what the Baron meant by watch and learn. Hell, I might have gone with that chauffeur, no questions asked. He had recognized the insignia on the duffel bag . . . and they were expecting to be picked up. Blake felt the trickle of perspiration down his neck. Working this end was nothing like the deals he had done for Iggy.

His thoughts were interrupted by a loud voice. "Welcome to Bogota, *amigos*." The cheerful greeting came from a large, robust fellow who introduced himself as Perfidio . . . but do not let the name fool you . . . it was a joke of my mother's to irritate my philandering father."

"And a very big one, at that," Eduardo quipped, as he sized him up.

"Senor Modena has instructed me to take you for an enjoyable ride in the countryside."

Blake looked at Eduardo who nodded in agreement. So far, so good. The three men exited the terminal. A sleek, black Mercedes awaited. There was someone seated in the front passenger seat. Perfidio introduced him as Senor Caceres. He was a rugged looking individual, intimidating, to say the least. Eduardo showed no reaction. Blake felt at ease.

"Relax, gentlemen, and enjoy the scenery. We have quite a ride to Medellin. Have a drink; enjoy the TV. We'll be there before you know it. Make yourselves comfortable."

The car had everything. Eduardo poured tequila shots with a splash of lemon.

"Here's mud in your eye," Blake toasted.

Eduardo gave him another one of his 'crazy American' appraisals, as he gulped down his drink.

They settled back in their seats, occasionally gazing out the windows at the passing countryside. Blake's mind wandered to Christine . . . how beautiful she is, how desirable. That lucky bastard Charles. Well, he'll get what he deserves when the right time comes.

The car came to a sudden halt. Blake, startled out of his reverie, looked out the window at a huge area of overgrown brush and trees. What the hell? We're out in the middle of nowhere. After a closer look, he calmed down, realizing that there was a cleared, trodden path over to the side.

Perfidio told them, "Gentlemen, from here you have a little walk. Bring your luggage. My friend will remain here with me to await your return."

As he exited the car, Blake saw two rifles which he hadn't noticed before, on the front seat. Everybody's packing but me.

Suddenly, Eduardo produced a small pistol and handed it to Blake. "Just in case . . ."

I've heard that song before, Blake thought, and placed the gun inside his jacket.

They walked straight ahead and soon came to a clearing in the woods . . . the airstrip. The sound of motors, faint in the distance, grew louder as a small plane came into view.

"Here they are," Eduardo said. "On your toes and follow my lead."

When the plane landed, three men in business attire, wearing dark glasses, disembarked. Each had the familiar bulge on the left side of his jacket. Two of them carried black leather suitcases.

Blake followed Eduardo as he approached them. The men with the suitcases came forward; the third kept a distance. "Good afternoon, gentlemen," one said. "I am Carlos Modena. How is the market these days?"

"Good as ever. As long as the *muchachas* stay hungry for dresses."

The third man spoke up. "Well said. Open the suitcases and the duffel bag. We will count the money; you two will count the 'tickets' and make the usual taste test.

No one spoke as the money and the kilos of cocaine were checked. All the while, the third man stood guard. Finally, with everything calculated to the satisfaction of all, the men shook hands with Blake and Eduardo and then boarded the plane. Take off was immediate.

Eduardo and Blake, heading back to the path, two suitcases in hand, hadn't gone very far when, suddenly, Perfifio and Caceres appeared from the underbrush. This startled Blake but not Eduardo.

"I see all went well," Perfidio said.

Back in the car, Eduardo urged Perfidio to get them to the airport as soon as possible. They wouldn't be stopping for dinner. "We have a plane to catch tonight."

Blake settled back in his seat. Piece of cake. I worried for nothing.

Clearance at the airport was easy. Some customs and baggage handlers were in the pockets of the Baron. After they boarded the plane and got comfortable, Blake turned to Eduardo. "Tell me, why were Perfidio and Caceres hiding in the underbrush?"

A poker-faced Eduardo responded, "They were there to kill you if you messed up . . . or to kill them, if the deal didn't go down right."

*   *   *

Back in Hollywood, Jim Green was still spending time on the Strip. He was almost finished with his article. Bill and Tony had served their purpose well. He'd also gotten chummy with some of the working girls and boys who proved to be fountains of information. Even the small pushers liked to chat with him. When he was winding down one night,

Jim casually mentioned to Bill, "I think I saw your friend Blake the other night. Guess he's back in town."

"Nah," Tony butt in. "He's in Mexico on movie business."

"Really?" Jim tried to hide how much this news interested him. "Guess he got a lucky break . . ."

Bill cut in. "We only know what the word is on the street . . . something one of the extras told one of the guys."

Jim played it cool. "Well, he had a pretty good deal doing for him here with Iggy, from what you told me. I'm surprised he gave it up to do a movie."

"Yeah. Iggy's still pissed," Tony said soberly. "Blake's move came down hard on Iggy's head. He's a nervous wreck lately."

"Why?" Jim asked.

"He doesn't know who Blake might be talking to . . . maybe a slip of the tongue, ya know . . . ?"

"Well, let's hope all his talking will be done on screen," Jim said.

Bill laughed. "You got that right."

"Sounds like Blake better watch his back." When that comment hit a wall of silence, Jim decided to go no further.

Bill and Tony seemed distracted by something going on close by. Suddenly, someone was running towards them.

Bill yelled, "Tony, Jim, run for cover."

The three of them bolted into the nearest hallway. They heard shots ring out and shouts on the street, followed by the sound of sirens. "Another night in Paradise," Bill said sarcastically. After a while, he peeked out the doorway. A body was being loaded into an ambulance. A couple of police cars pulled away. "Something went down tonight."

They walked out of the hallway to the street. Bill approached two men who Jim recognized as pushers. "Yeah," one of them said, "they knocked off Chico; inside job. He was wheeling and dealing on the side and Iggy got wind of it. The fix was in after that. Chico should have known better but the big bucks blinded him."

"Happens all the time," Bill observed.

As the three of them strolled down the Strip, Jim decided that now was the time to tell Bill and Tony that he wasn't going to be coming around anymore. "I have to do this. Gotta get off the stuff. It's interfering with my job. You guys have been good company. Maybe see you around sometime."

Tony looked at Jim, surprised. "Ya think ya ain't gonna need a sniff once in a while? Ya gonna try to go cold turkey? Never happen."

Bill was more practical. Nothing surprised him. "Good luck, Jim. If you need us, you know where to find us."

Jim nodded. "So long, guys." He could hardly wait to get to his phone. Wait until Charles hears who's in Mexico City.

*   *   *

THE FLAWLESS MISTRESS wrapped within Mr. V.'s expectations, thanks to the weather holding up. A happy cast and crew would be heading back to L.A.—except for Charles and Christine. They planned to drive to the villa by the sea which they had rented.

Mr. V. congratulated everyone and, especially, his stars. "Christine and Russ, you were wonderful to work with. We have a sure fire hit on our hands. See you in a couple of weeks at the screening."

Russ Crowell shook his hand. "It's been a pleasure."

Christine hugged Mr. V., kissing him on both cheeks. "Thank you so much for the privilege of working with you."

Turning to Russ, she said, "And to you, Russ, thanks for all your support."

He embraced her. "You were just fine to work with, lovely lady. See you in L.A."

Goodbyes said and done, Christine and Charles gathered their luggage and rushed over to their limo. "Oh, Charlie, I can't believe it. My first movie, finished, and now I'm going to have you all to myself for two weeks."

At that moment, Charles' cell phone rang. Jim's excited voice at the other end said, "Would you believe? I heard Blake's involved in a movie in Mexico City . . ."

"No way." Charles moved out of earshot. "There is no other movie in the works here. Who told you that?"

Jim recounted one of his last conversations with the boys on LaBrea. Charles voiced his doubts.

"Well, I'll be on it. Call you as soon as I find out anything more."

"Thanks, Jim. You're a pal. We're off now for our little vacation. I'm not saying anything about this to Chris. It would only ruin things. Keep in touch and thanks again." He clicked off.

What in hell was Blake Dugan doing in Mexico!

The villa was everything they'd hoped it would be: private beach and all. Christine was so happy. Charles was determined that no bad news was going to spoil their respite.

As soon as they unpacked, Christine suggested, "Let's go for a swim. The water's so inviting." She was like a child in a toy shop, touching everything as she danced around shedding her clothes on the furniture, the floor, or wherever they landed as she gleefully tossed them about.

Charles laughed at her antics as he began to disrobe. Then holding her irresistible body in his arms, he carried her out on the sand, all the while whispering how much he loved her.

"Race you to the water," she shouted as she pulled out of his embrace.

Like two carefree children, they dashed to the water's edge and jumped in.

Circumstances were idyllic as the sun sank and a cool breeze hovered over them. After enjoying their frolicking and a good swim, they wrapped themselves in a huge beach towel and lay down under an umbrella large enough to afford them the privacy to make love with abandon.

For two weeks, they wined and dined, sometimes in quaint little restaurants, but mostly alone in their villa. There were a few afternoons when they would browse the colorful little shops in the area. "I'm big on souvenirs," Christine said, "and I want something I can always look at and remember our special time here."

Charles couldn't refuse her. She was like a child when she wanted something, delightfully petulant but lovable. As they strolled in and out of quaint shops, Charles felt uneasy, thinking that Blake could be lurking anywhere. Meanwhile, Christine found several items she "just had to have."

Christine interrupted his thoughts. Examining some 'sandalias', she said, "Aren't these sandals adorable? I think I'll get them in a few colors. What do you think?" When Charles didn't respond, he voice went up an octave. "Charlie, are you listening?"

"Sure, Honey. I'm sorry, I guess my mind was wandering." He looked at the sandals in her hand. "They look great. Get a few pair."

Christine frowned. "Charlie, since we got here, I've had the feeling, now and then, that your mind is on another planet. Is anything wrong?"

"Chris, everything is just great. I want it all to be perfect for you so sometimes I get lost in thoughts about what else I can do for you."

"You're a sweetheart—but stop thinking so much. You've already made my life perfection. I'm the luckiest girl in the universe." She gave him a dazzling smile. "Okay, now . . . what colors?"

CHAPTER FOURTEEN

I t was pitch black on the Miami waters as a ship eased its way carrying more then five hundred shirts (more than $500,000 worth of cocaine), wrapped in burlap bags.

With its lights out, a sleek black car slid silently down the deserted beach into a remote area of the Port's loading docks. Eduardo and Blake watched in silence as the sound of a motor purred softly and a small, two-cabin cruiser approached. The ship cut its motors as it pulled in close to shore. Within moments, a flashlight flickered several times.

"Okay," Eduardo said. "Grab the valise and wait until we get the signal to board."

"Right on." Blake's voice did not betray his unavoidable apprehension, having never participated in this type of transaction. His mind raced. For all they knew, they could be facing the U. S. Coast Guard. Stranger things have happened in this crazy business—and there were the body bags to prove it. A few more flickers of a flashlight and Eduardo nudged Blake forward. "All aboard, mate."

After the customary exchange of code words, they unloaded the product from the blister on the side of the ship. Blisters were a new wrinkle. Smugglers hid their drugs in a blister, a compartment added to the outside of the ship, so that if they were approached by the Coast Guard, the blister could be easily disposed of by detaching it and allowing it to fall into the water.

There was little conversation. Blake watched as Eduardo handled the deal with ease.

Observing the characters involved, Blake thought that if this wasn't a drug deal, he'd swear these guys were actors in a cops-and-robbers B movie.

Eduardo signaled him that they were leaving. They picked up the burlap bags and hastened to their car.

As the cruiser edged out into deeper water, one of the men remarked, "You know, the *gringo* looks familiar. It's hard to place him because of the mustache and beard, but I could swear I have seen him before . . . under different circumstances."

"They all look alike when they grow facial hair," the other replied.

"Perhaps so. Let's get out of here *pronto*."

As Eduardo started the car, they heard the ship's motor humming full speed ahead. Blake settled back in his seat. His mind was on the deal just completed. He, too, had experienced the feeling that he had seen one of the men elsewhere. But where? LaBrea? One of Iggy's . . ." This gave him a jolt.

*   *   *

Back at the mansion, the Baron expressed his satisfaction. "You did well. I think it is time for you, Blake, to meet with some of our South American contractors. They will be arriving soon in Los Angeles."

Blake welcomed the news. His stygian thoughts lately had put him into a funk. A visit to L.A. was just what he needed.

The Baron lit a cigar, offered one to Blake, and poured them two whiskies. They clinked glasses. Blake waited patiently. The Baron relished a few puffs on his Cuban then continued. "A suite has been reserved for you at the Century Plaza under the name of Jaime Calderone. The only people who will know this name are you and the reps of the South American cartel . . . one of our big suppliers. You will have appropriate charge cards and a good supply of cash."

"When do I leave? And how long will I be staying?"

"You fly to L.A. International next Friday, eleven a.m., for three days. The contractors will arrive at the hotel at five p.m. that evening. Be a gracious host. Have fine wine and hors d'oeuvres delivered to your suite. It's nice to do business while you enjoy the fruits of your labor. Of course, you will bring a box of the best Cubans with you."

Blake felt like he had just been awarded an Oscar. But, he did realize that if he screwed up, the penalty would be far more deadly than a critic's bad review.

The Baron continued to instruct him in the art of the deal. Blake's mind was racing, contemplating an opportunity to check on Christine.

The Baron was saying, "That evening, if things are going smoothly, take your guests out for a good time. You know the town well, eh? . . . some clubs, some girls . . ."

"No problem," Blake assured him. "I know L.A. like a book. They will have a memorable night."

"Good. I am anxious to develop strong ties with these people before my competitors move in. If the deal is closed before the weekend is over and they leave, you have the rest of the time for yourself. Just make sure you take the midnight flight back on Sunday. Eduardo will be at the airport to pick you up."

Blake couldn't believe his luck. Fan-freakin-tastic! "Baron, thank you for your confidence. I won't disappoint you."

"I know you won't." The Baron snuffed out the stump of his cigar. "Good luck."

*   *   *

Iggy stood huddled in the doorway of a bruised and battered building on Spring and Second Streets that bore all the markings and ravages of the gang wars that were so much a part of life on Skid Row in Downtown L.A. His attaché case was gripped firmly in his left hand as his eyes scanned the dingy street and its occupants. All around him were hustlers, prostitutes, and cruising gang members looking for trouble. He fingered the holster underneath his jacket. "I hate this whole freakin' scene," he muttered. "Shoulda sent one of my mules." But, the money he netted from doing these small street deals himself was too tempting.

Within moments, two weird looking teens swaggered up to him. Jesus, Iggy thought, would you look at the get up on these guys and the tattoos.

The taller of the two demanded, "You the candyman?"

"Yeah. Why?"

"Got some good candy for us?"

Iggy squirmed, annoyed. "Let's see the dough first."

"Got it right here, man."

The metal of a revolver glistened in the dark as shots rang out. Iggy didn't see it coming. His right hand had barely reached his gun. His left hand was still clutching the attaché case. Blood oozed from his chest. He managed to squeeze off two shots before he fell to the pavement. From where he lay, Iggy could see the bodies of the two boys sprawled on the pavement. His bullets had reached their marks. "You don't mess with me, you little shits." That was the last thought Iggy would ever have.

Police and ambulances cordoned off the area within minutes. The bodies were placed in body bags and loaded onto ambulances. The Medical Examiner had his work cut out for him. It would be a busy night at the Coroner's Office on No. Mission Road.

For the L.A.P.D., it was just another night Downtown.

*   *   *

Only the habitués of LaBrea could appreciate how important this hit was—especially Bill and Tony. They knew the repercussions Iggy's murder could bring: a drug turf war. Iggy had always managed to ward off anything like that. He was well connected.

"Damn those gangs. We had it under control until they began getting into the act," Tony grumbled as he punched the wall nearest him.

Bill laughed. "No use breaking your arm over it . . . and, tell me, just what in hell did **we** have under control?"

"Well, nuthin' . . . but these kids piss me off. Why don't they stick to their lootin' and gang wars and stuff like that?"

Bill was annoyed. "Shut up. We got a lot of thinking to do. Wonder who'll take Iggy's place? He played it pretty straight with us. As long as he got his money, no hassle. Who knows who we'll have to deal with now." He shook his head.

As it turned out, there was a peaceful transition of power. The man that Iggy had reported to approached Bill one night. "Hear you're a good man around here. Iggy liked you . . . spoke well of you. Interested in moving up?"

"Sure." Bill was cool.

So the mantle was passed. Tony was a happy fellow. He kept repeating, "You the man" to Bill, who finally told him to "knock it off" but, he couldn't help suppressing a smile.

*   *   *

Blake was in town the day after Iggy was shot. His appointment with the contractors wasn't until five p.m. when they were to meet at the Century Plaza. They would ask for Mr. Calderone's room where Blake would be waiting. These appointments were arranged in different places. Blake had to be particularly covert. His face was familiar to some desk clerks because of his past activities but the recent addition of his long mustache and chin hair seemed to do the trick.

He learned about the shoot-out from Ernie, an acquaintance he ran into at one of the local diners where he was having lunch. The place was a favorite of low echelon movie people. Blake decided to eat there instead of at the hotel because he hoped to get an update on Christine. Ernie didn't recognize Blake at first, who explained to him that he was playing a role in a movie, hence the facial hair. After some small talk, Ernie asked, "Didn't you once date Christine O'Hara?"

"Yes. Why?" Blake was immediately on edge.

"Well, she certainly has done fabulously well for herself. Has a sure fire hit on her hands and I hear she'd being considered for the lead in a blockbuster that's in the works. She'll be starring with Russ Crowell again. It can't miss."

"What about THE FLAWLESS MISTRESS? That should be opening soon"

"You know the drill," Ernie said. "After the Premiere, it'll go to a few select theatres and then go nationwide. The word is it's a smash."

Blake's facial muscles were twitching. The lucky bitch. "Good for her." His voice did not reveal his rancor. Keeping cool, he said, "Well, Ernie, maybe we'll run into each other at a casting call. Nice seeing you. Good luck."

The news of Iggy's demise had been a shock, at first, but then Blake felt a wave of relief. No more worries about retribution. Now, back to Christine . . . He hopped into his rental and headed for Beverly Hills. Got some time on my hands. Why not check out the lovebirds, he thought. The blood rushed to his head as he clenched the wheel. "I sure hope you enjoyed your vacation," he muttered as he floored the accelerator.

He drove slowly down their street, stopping occasionally as though looking for an address. At one point, a resident approached the car. "May I help you? What address are you looking for?"

Blake didn't appreciate the questions. He made some insipid remark and quickly moved on. I could swear I worked in a film with that guy. Now, in broad daylight, Blake was able to get a better look at the house with its oversized driveway, garage, and beautifully, sculptured landscaping. Not bad, he observed. He checked his wristwatch. Better get going. Just enough time to get back to the hotel, shower, dress and arrange for his guests.

Driving back, he felt enthusiastic about the evening. It'll be good to take the contractors out on the town, and a little extra-curricular activity on his home turf was just what he needed.

The evening went well. Excellent cuisine, the best liquor and fine cigars led to satisfactory agreements and a handshake.

"Now, gentlemen," Blake said, "let's go out to some of the hottest spots in L.A. I'm sure you will find some desirable companions to fulfill your wishes." He winked broadly.

His suggestions were greeted with enthusiasm. The night went well and by three a.m. they returned to the hotel, each with a more than willing companion by the arm. Before they hastened to their rooms, they agreed to meet for lunch at one p.m., in the Hotel Café. One of the men told Blake, "We will be flying out this afternoon. Thank you for a splendid evening of pleasure and diversion."

"The pleasure was all mine," Blake responded. And more so, he thought. I have the rest of the weekend to myself.

CHAPTER FIFTEEN

After their return to L.A., Christine and Charles were on a merry-go-round of meetings and readings with her agent/publicist and the producers of the proposed work, DESIRE. Christine read for the lead: Jessica, a woman with a deep love for her man, struggling to escape the vengeful actions of a rejected suitor. Her 'man' would be played by Russ Crowell; the role of the villain, by Johnny Drew. Once again, they would be under the direction of Mr. V.

"Oh, Charlie, this is so wonderful, playing opposite Russ again, and with that fab actor, Johnny Drew. And you know how much I love Mr. V." She inhaled deeply.

"Hey, young lady, don't forget the cinematographer," Charles teased. "Mr. V. already has me on hold."

"That makes it all perfect . . . the way you always want it to be for me. I love you, Charles Markham. Let's go home and celebrate."

After dinner, they sat on their patio quietly enjoying a glass of champagne in the cool, night air. The dark sky was a suitable backdrop for the brilliant array of stars.

"The stars seem unusually close tonight, Charlie. Dozens of them. When I was a little girl, I wished upon them every night. I guess all girls do." Suddenly, she pointed out one star. "Charlie, look! I feel like it's winking at me, saying, 'I'm your special star, Christine.' Isn't it beautiful?"

Charles looked at her radiant face as moonlight graced it and highlighted her stunning features. "Sweet Christine, that's the evening star and it **is** your special star. It's the first to shine, shines the brightest and shines the longest."

She hugged him and he could tell she was silently making a wish.

*   *   *

The next morning, over breakfast, Christine commented. "Funny, that his new film is the story of love and rejection. Sound familiar?"

"It's a case of art imitating life, Chris."

"Been there, done that," she answered wryly. "No wonder I gave it such a good read. I'm living it." Suddenly, she laughed. "I can't help thinking that Blake would be perfect in the role of the rejected suitor. Wouldn't that be a hoot?"

Charles had other ideas about Blake. He changed the subject. "We've got a whole day to ourselves. What's on tap?" He pulled her close and felt the warmth envelop his eyes and course through his body.

"Get your running shoes on, Charlie. I'll race you to the bedroom."

"Ready, set . . ." He beat her to the bed and pulled her down upon him as she came scooting over, a split second behind.

After an afternoon of relaxation and pure pleasure, they decided to have an early meal and watch TV. While they were eating, Charles suddenly asked, "Chris, would you mind if I called Jim and met with him for a couple of hours?"

She pouted, "I thought we'd have one of those rare evenings at home . . ." She flashed him a smile. "Of course, Charlie. I don't mind. It'll be good for both of you to spend some time together. I'll just enjoy a long soak in the tub . . ."

"That conjures up an image that could make me change my mind." He hesitated a moment. "I'd better call him now."

*   *   *

They met at their favorite place—the Pub. Jim spoke first. "Sorry, it didn't work out with Blake. I was hoping to nail the bastard for you, but he seemed to have disappeared—but I did get a good story."

"Good for you, Jim. I'm glad. But, I just can't help wondering what the Blake Mexican connection was all about. Sure as hell wasn't a movie. I heard some scuttlebutt on the set. A bit player was telling a couple of cast members that he noticed Blake one day watching an outdoor shot of MISTRESS. If he's up to his old tricks, I'll kill the bastard," Charles was fuming.

"You know," Jim said, "he left a bad taste in the mouths of some of his cronies downtown. Maybe they'll do the job for you."

"I'll drink to that." Charles raised his glass. "To Blake's final curtain."

"Speaking of final curtains, the dealer that Blake was connected with was shot and killed during a drug deal with some gang members. He managed to repay the compliment before he hit the pavement. Bloody mess."

"Too bad Blake wasn't at the end of one of those bullets."

Jim studied his friend carefully as Charles gulped down another scotch and soda. His demeanor was beginning to worry Jim. "Charlie, you wouldn't try anything irrational . . . it's not worth it. Blake'll get his just desserts one of these days."

"He sure will," Charles agreed. He signaled Tim for another round. "Here's to the blindfolded lady holding the scales."

Jim was worried. He never saw Charles drink this much and in such a mood. "Let's get a burger and call it a night. I've still got that eight a.m. roll call at the newspaper."

It was close to two a.m. when they said their goodnights and got into their cars. "God, I hope he doesn't do anything stupid," Jim murmured as he waved to Charles.

*   *   *

The weeks that followed were filled with photo-ops and meetings. Christine felt rejuvenated and eager to get 'into character'. Meanwhile, all of Tinseltown awaited the premiere of THE FLAWLESS MISTRESS. The PR and hype had the town buzzing. Finally, with the usual Hollywood fanfare, the film opened at Grauman's Chinese. The biggest names in filmdom trod the red carpet. Fans, shouting their approval, lined the streets and entranceways.

This is something Hollywood does best. It puts talent on parade in the finest creations by top couturieres, wearing the most fabulous jewelry that Winston's can provide for the event. Christine looked ravishing in a Grecian draped, smoky grey chiffon strapless gown that hugged her body. Gathered at her bosom, a cluster of white fresh water pearls. Matching dangles of pearls hung from each ear. A mother-of-pearl evening bag and grey silk sandals completed the vision.

As the floodlights picked up Christine's entrance, a roar went up from the fans. She held Charles' hand tightly. "Don't let go, Charlie or I'm sure I'll fall on my face," she said, through clenched teeth beneath smiling lips. "This is surreal."

His broad smile reflected his pride in her. "This moment in time is yours to cherish. So fasten your seat belt, Honey, it's going to be a grand night."

Christine tried not to laugh. "Shades of Bette Davis," she whispered, "but not exactly."

The rest of the night was like a dream sequence. When the film ended, her peers gave it a standing ovation. As they were leaving, members of the movie community milled about her, offering congratulations.

In their limo, on the way home, Christine broke down in tears. "Tears of joy, Charlie."

He held her in his arms. "Let it all hang out, Baby. You've earned it."

*   *   *

Blake Dugan was on a plane back to Mexico the night THE FLAWLESS MISTRESS opened at Grauman's. He was aware of all the publicity and was tempted to stay another night to catch a glimpse of Christine, but he knew better than to change plans. He was expected at the airport in Mexico City and would be there. Blake didn't want anything to interfere with his relationship with the Baron. Got a real soft touch there, he mused. Life at the mansion was better than good. Most evenings were spent wining and dining luxuriously with the beautiful women who graced their table. And, Blake, never had a problem bedding down the one of his choice. Rosa, an actress in a local stage company, was his special companion. As far as the others were concerned, they were a couple.

When Blake told the Baron what he had heard of Iggy's murder, the Baron became quiet . . . thoughtful. After a few minutes, he said, "You know, this may open new doors for us. It is too bad about Iggy. He was a good associate. This gang business interests me. I have some thinking to do about an idea in my head that may interest you."

Blake nodded. Oh, shit, I hope he's not thinking of getting me involved Downtown. The scene there was growing worse. Undercover cops, dressed in scruffy clothes, masqueraded as street dealers. There were massive drug busts on Skid Row. The place was in a perpetual rhythm of Mardi Gras time on crack, which was sold in full view. Hustlers, gangsters, addicts, narcos roamed the streets and turf wars escalated. Arrests and incarcerations increased and the police hoped to discourage outsiders from seeking supplies there. Blake had seen and heard enough. He knew this would be a long haul for the authorities and he didn't want to be a part of it.

The Baron's voice interrupted his thoughts. "What do you think about making connections with the top dog gang? If we play our cards right, we can take over. We will promise them the best, in quantity. They can take over the streets, but we will be in control. They will dance to our music."

Blake did not betray his feelings. He knew better. "Baron, to do this we have to devise a plan that will always keep the gangs in place."

"In place? When we explain the deal and lay down the rules, I don't think they will mess with us. We can always show them what that means, to stay in place, eh?"

"You are right, Baron." Blake knew what 'show them' meant. "How do you plan to take control?"

"We have effective ways, my boy. How do you think my cartel survives? Blake, I want you to spend some time Downtown. Find out which gangs dominate and which one is the strongest. Then we will put a plan in place."

Blake remained poker faced. Well, he thought, there is a positive to all this. He'd be spending more time nearer to Christine. "When do we start?"

"You'll hear from me shortly." He bid Blake goodnight.

Blake went to look for Rosa.

A day later, the Baron sent for Blake who had spent the last twenty-four hours with Rosa, drinking tequila and making love—and not necessarily in that order. When Eduardo knocked on his bedroom door, Blake yelled. "Be out in a minute." He knew that special knock—triple staccato—meant out on the double.

Eduardo knew Blake's minute would be ten or so. "No problem." After all, the man had to shower and dress. He returned to the sitting room and advised the Baron. "Blake will be here shortly. He has had a busy night."

The Baron laughed, winking broadly, as he continued to puff on his cigar. "He is quite the lover, is he not?"

Eduardo nodded. A smile played about his lips.

When Blake entered the room, the men were both joking about Blake's growing reputation as a ladies' man. He thought he caught the tale end of something to that effect. "Good day. How is everyone?"

"Fine." The Baron smiled. "I see you look well satisfied. Had a good night's sleep?"

"Uh, yeah, sure." Blake wondered, What the hell is this nonsense? "You sent for me, Baron?"

The Baron motioned for Eduardo to take his leave then he turned to Blake. "You know, Blake, I have had palmy days in this business. For a long time, my business with people in the Golden Triangle in the Sierra Madre and my sources overseas have been excellent; my customers, countless. But, my boy, there is always room for more money to be made."

Blake sat motionless, waiting.

"You know, *la daya*, the D.E.A., is gradually narrowing down the field. Law enforcement is constantly involved in sting operations to stop the flow of drugs into the United States. Of course, they are not 100% successful, but they make a big dent in the business.

"And, it is getting bloodier all the time. So much fighting for control. The drug lords favor smaller cartels because it is safer and more profitable to deal with less people. Often, it is necessary to eliminate someone. This we do by planned executions, usually drive-by shootings."

Blake felt a chill run down his body. He didn't like to hear about that side of the business. He waited patiently for the Baron to come to the point. What the devil was he leading up to?

Finally, the Baron said, "This news of gangs involved in dealing drugs Downtown interests me. I understand the dealers and pushers on the street are cleaning up. I want to change that, to get that action. It's time to get rid of the little man. You will find out which are the strongest gangs and establish contact with them."

Blake's mind was racing. He was comfortable in his short sojourns to L.A. and the high end benefits. This proposal puts him in less desirable circumstances.

The Baron observed Blake's eyes darting back and forth. "Blake," he continued, "you will make more money you have ever dreamed of, I promise you."

Blake heard the magic word. His greed engine kicked in. Maybe this is just what I need. The Baron's voice interrupted his thoughts.

"You will handle deliveries, dealing directly with the top dogs of the gangs."

"Baron, please explain the supply chain so that I have a clear picture of what my role is."

The Baron smiled at Blake's 'role' reference. Ever the actor. "All right. We will do this point by point. You will go Downtown, rent a warehouse (this will be your stash house) and set up an office there. You will have a crew of men who will drive the trucks which will be equipped with hidden compartments. For all purposes, these trucks will be delivering parts and equipment for TV sets."

Blake was about to say something, but the Baron continued. "Of course, you must select the gang members we will deal with. Investigate them thoroughly. Choosing the wrong ones could result in a turf war . . . and we don't want another Iggy fiasco. Try to stay off the street as much as possible. Have them come to you. In the warehouse, you will always have cover. If there is ever a problem, yell "No turkey Thanksgiving" and your men will draw their guns and, if necessary, shoot to kill. In this business, you must think fast and act even faster."

Blake drew his breath in sharply. This was a hell of a lot more than he bargained for. Shoot outs were not his forte but there was no turning back now . . . his greed and ego quickly overcame his reticence.

The Baron was speaking again. "Remember, Blake, point by point. Oh, yes, get rid of the mustached and beard. While I like you looking like one of us, now you must look like a *gringo* again. It will sit better with the Yankee gangs, I think. A haircut would help, too"

This advice startled Blake. He enjoyed being incognito.

The Baron was waiting for an answer. "Well, my friend, do we have a handshake on it? Of course, there are many details to work out, so we will speak again very soon. Meanwhile, fly up to L.A. and scout the territory."

"Done." Blake extended his hand.

"Good. Let's drink to our new enterprise." The Baron snapped his fingers and shouted for Eduardo. "Champagne, *pronto*!"

CHAPTER SIXTEEN

When Blake arrived at L.A. International, he hailed a cab and went directly to the Century Plaza. He had every intention of enjoying the benefits of his assignment. The Baron had given him carte blanche, "but, use your discretion wisely".

To the clerk behind the desk, a driver's license identified Blake as Sean Ferguson. A bedroom suite had been reserved for him. A bellhop took care of his luggage. Blake flipped him a twenty dollar bill. The look of appreciation on the boy's face and his excessive thanks flattered Blake's vanity.

He settled in and called for room service. "Send up an order of orange juice, eggs Benedict, white toast and coffee. Thanks." He phoned the concierge requesting a car, specifically a white convertible Mercedes. If nothing else, Blake had a nose for style. He finished breakfast, had an exhilarating shower and changed into casual attire.

In the lobby, he picked up a copy of the L.A. Times, got comfortable in one of the large armchairs and proceeded to check out the real estate section for available warehouse rentals. After earmarking a few potentials, he headed for the hotel garage.

He pointed the nose of the Mercedes toward the heart of the City. Gotta check out The Strip, was his first thought. He loved the dazzling collection of clubs and restaurants. As he drove around, he recalled good times there. The working girls and guys were out in full force, and not too far away were the "feel good" hustlers. Same old, same old.

It was a drive Downtown to the first address he had circled in the Classified Ads. Out front was a sign displaying an agent's name and phone number. Blake checked out the street. "Looking good," he observed, out loud. "Just what the doctor ordered—decrepit and full of sleazy characters, either high on drugs or wheeling and dealing them." On the corner, he watched a young fellow score a drug deal while his sidekick was already strung out on blow. Blake smiled. Good show. Keep the bucks coming. This area is right for the operation. He would be the main honcho. But, let's not forget that the Baron is number one.

His eyes scanned the area for any other persons of interest. Blake had been forewarned about ATF agents, posing as drug dealers, doing surveillance on street gangs that were gradually controlling narcotics trafficking. His gaze fell upon two men hanging out on the corner. Could be, but right now, not important.

He checked out the other real estate leads, but none proved more suitable than the first one he had looked at. When he returned to his suite, he called the number he had jotted down.

"Best Value Realty," a cheerful voice answered. "This is Donna. How may I help you?"

"Donna, this is Sean Ferguson. I'm a businessman interested in renting a small warehouse. I saw your sign at Central Avenue and 6th Street and would like to see the place. When is that possible?"

"I'd be happy to meet with you. Is tomorrow afternoon convenient? I can be there at one-thirty."

"Fine. I'll see you then." Blake hung up. Well, that's a start. He glanced at his wristwatch. Four-thirty. Cocktail time. He called room service. After a couple of drinks, I'll go back to the Strip and enjoy supper in one of my favorite haunts. Blake frowned suddenly, recalling the night at the Irish Pub when the bartender had thrown him out. Well, one of these days, I'll even that score. He'll eat his words.

A bellhop delivered the hors d'oeuvres and the bottle of champagne Blake had ordered. For the next couple of hours, he relaxed. At seven p.m., he showered again and dressed in what he considered appropriate for a night on The Strip: A casual tee shirt, jeans, and Nike's. For the moment, incognito was the word. He had been able to convince the Baron that he should retain the long mustache. "It's good cover," Blake insisted . . . the less recognizable, the better.

*   *   *

When it came to women, Blake's philosophy was "grab it whenever and wherever you can." Fate is the hunter and he always bagged his prey. It was now two a.m. and he was sloshed after making the rounds. Sitting next to him in his final stop was a voluptuous, striking looking young thing who was all over him, like white on rice.

At closing time, Blake suggested she join him for a nightcap at his hotel. She was more than happy to do so. The nightcap evolved into a marathon of sex ending at dawn. The last thing a sober Blake wanted now was company.

"Okay, Babe, get showered and dressed."

She started to say something cute and tried to embrace him. Blake, annoyed, reacted by pushing her roughly away. "Quit while you're ahead, Bimbo. Get your ass out of here!"

The girl was shocked. She hadn't figured him for this sort. He had been so romantic all night. Now he frightened her. His handsome face was distorted into a mask of anger. "Okay, okay," she whimpered. She washed up and dressed as quickly as she could.

"Well, so long," she said hesitantly.

Blake held the door open. He shoved a $100 dollar bill into her hand and slammed the door behind her. His mind was racing. Gotta take a nap, shower, have some lunch and head over to meet the realtor at one-thirty. Typical Blake, he wondered what she looked like.

Blake stood in front of the warehouse at exactly one thirty p.m. No agent in sight. Where the hell was she? Blake was a creature of time, knowing from experience the difference even a minute can make. Well, no sweat, he told himself.

Within five minutes, a Chrysler convertible pulled up to the curb. The first thing Blake noticed was a long, shapely pair of legs extending from the open door. His glance quickly traveled up a curvaceous body to a beautiful face framed by coiffed blonde tresses.

"Mr. Ferguson? Donna Golden of True Value Realty." She shook his hand.

Blake, whose mind had reached another dimension for the moment, had to adjust his concentration. "Pleased to meet you, Donna."

"Let's go inside. I'll show you around and answer any question you may have." She handed him a printed sheet. "Here's a copy of the specs. It provides all the basic information. I'll fill in the rest." She flashed him a friendly smile.

Blake quietly checked the specs and then looked carefully around. Not bad. Roomy bay area, office in the back—even a small kitchen and toilet facilities. Perfect for a stash house, he decided. He asked questions about the length of the lease, the area around the warehouse, and restrictions about trucking deliveries and pick up times.

"You may conduct your business as necessary. I'm sure there won't be a problem, Mr. Ferguson. It's not like you're going to carry on some illegal activities. TV parts—what harm could there be in that?" She laughed.

"Everything seems satisfactory. I'm interested. What's the next step?"

"We'll go to my office and firm up the deal. I'll need a deposit and references."

"Fine. Upward and onward." He followed her to her office.

Blake had everything in place. The Baron had anticipated every requirement should Blake find something suitable. He had a list of companies with whom he would be doing business and he was able to write a check for the first two months of a twelve month lease, with option to renew. She gave him the keys and they shook hands.

Donna was a happy camper. It wasn't always easy to rent or sell property Downtown because of all the gang and drug problems.

When the papers were signed, sealed and delivered, Blake said, "Donna, I thank you so much for all your help." He checked his watch. "It's almost dinner time, may I have the pleasure . . ."

She cut him short, apologetically. "I would love to, but I have plans for this evening. Can we make it another time?" Donna found him attractive. He was no doubt well heeled. Why not?

Blake felt shot down, but said, "Too bad. How about tomorrow night?"

"Terrific."

Blake liked her style. No cute stuff. No games. Right to the point. "Speak with you in the a.m." He flashed her a winning smile.

She smiled back. He sure is handsome. Hope he has a personality to match, she thought, as she got behind the wheel of her car and accelerated.

* * *

Blake was pleased with himself. Not a bad day's work. The Baron will be happy to learn of his progress. Tomorrow he would go back Downtown and check out the street people—but, right now, it's time for another evening of relaxation. He was in a good mood as he changed from his smart sport jacket and slacks to his 'Strip persona' attire. Taking inventory in the mirror, he said to his image, "Who knows? You might get lucky, lover boy." He called down to the concierge and asked that his car be at the hotel entrance within ten minutes. No sense shlepping to the garage if he didn't have to.

He got downstairs just as the car was pulling up in front. Blake recognized the bellhop as the one who had handled his luggage. I'll wow him again. Blake said, "Here you go, Junior." He handed the boy another twenty dollar bill and hopped into the driver's seat feeling satisfied with himself. "There's nothing like having big bucks to throw around. It sure gets you respect," he said to his image in the rear view mirror.

The previous night, his mind had turned briefly to his past humiliation at the Pub. Tonight, it crossed his mind again. He decided to drop in for supper and a drink and wondered if Tim would recognize him. This will be a good test.

Blake pulled in to the back parking lot, locked the car and walked into the Pub. Rather than sit at the bar, he decided to take a booth so he could check things out from a vantage point. Yep, same old Tim, plus another barkeep and a waitress. He recognized a few people at the bar. The waitress took his order—Irish Stew and a tankard of beer. Blake got up to go to the men's room, a move he knew would be noticed by the vigilant Tim. This will tell it all. He strolled over to the small hallway where a sign on the wall indicated "Rest Rooms". So far, so good.

As Tim glanced around the room, he observed what he thought looked like a new patron going to the 'john'. He watched later as Blake returned to his booth. "Maybe I should welcome him, make him feel at home," he remarked to his assistant. "Cover the bar."

Blake's dinner arrived at the same time Tim did. The waitress said, "If there's anything else you need, just give me a holler."

Keeping his head turned, Blake answered, "Everything looks great. Thanks."

Tim spoke up. "Good evening, Sir, Don't let me disturb your meal. I just wanted to welcome you. New here? Name's Tim."

Blake turned ever so slightly. "Thanks. Glad to meet you." He resumed eating.

When Tim returned behind the bar, he said, "Well, that wasn't the warmest reaction in the books. The guy barely looked at me. Funny . . . ya know, for a second there, I thought he looked familiar, but . . ." He shrugged.

"Hey, Tim, how's about a refill here?" It was one of his regulars.

"You got it, Sheila." Tim poured some lime juice, a generous shot of vodka, and some ice into a shaker. "One super vodka gimlet comin' up."

Blake sighed with relief. His new hair cut and long mustache must have done it. Tim hadn't shown the slightest recognition. He ate the rest of his meal with gusto, gulped down another beer or two and asked for the check. The waitress obliged and received a generous tip for her trouble.

As Blake made his way out the back exit, Tim glanced at him briefly. "Where have I seen that guy before?" He scratched his head and turned back to his customers.

It was a fun evening for Blake even though he opted not to bring home a companion. He decided on some decent shuteye. Going Downtown in the morning. Better be on your toes, old boy.

An old adage espouses that a person without a conscience has no trouble sleeping. Blake slept well.

*   *   *

At nine a.m., he was ready for his debut as the new man on Central and 6th. He loved role playing so he dressed 'tough' for the occasion. Before he left, he made the call to Donna Golden. "We on for tonight, Gorgeous?"

"Who is this please?" A girl can't be too careful.

"It's Sean Ferguson."

"Oh, Mr. Ferguson. Yes, I'm free this evening." She waited for him to speak again.

"Good. What do you say to six o'clock cocktails at Ivy's . . . and then dinner, place of your choice."

"Sounds great. Meet you at the bar at six." She liked the idea of meeting her dates. It made a getaway easy, if necessary.

"See you then, Darlin'." He hung up.

Driving with the top down, Blake found the fresh, late morning air exhilarating. He had good vibes about the day. For the most part, he was never one to feel inadequate. He wheeled the car into the driveway of the warehouse and sat for a few minutes, motor running, while he scanned the street. It was alive with crack heads and pushers, some doing deals; some already strung out.

It was obvious who the pushers were—the gang members, noticeable by their tattoos and their weird accessories. Blake lit a cigarette, puffing slowly, as he continued to watch the activity before him. Suddenly, a scuffle broke out, followed by loud shouts, expletives and gun shots. Two young men who he had figured for gang members were running in his direction. Blake quickly shut off the car. He fingered his gun. As they neared the warehouse, he called to them. "Hey, guys, in here." These punks could be just what he was looking for. They had all the earmarks.

Blake unlocked the side door to the warehouse and was quickly followed in by the two teenagers, one of whom still had a gun in his hand.

"What was that all about? Somebody step on your turf?" Blake asked.

The boys eyed him quizzically. "What's it to you?" the one with the gun asked. They exchanged glances. Who was this dude? He showed no fear. "What's on your mind?"

"Name's Ferguson. Let's just say I'm a connected guy looking to set up business here and it just might interest you. Let's talk. You'll be cool with it, I'm sure. But, first, what do I call you?"

One of the boys answered. "I'm Diego and this is Alex. So? Say what you hafta say. We're listening."

Blake thought, Tough little bastards. This is like a scene from a low budget movie, only it's for real. His gun resting against his left side gave him some comfort but he knew he needed the right words to accomplish what he had in mind. After some conversation and satisfied that he could do business with them, Blake carefully explained about filling orders for narcotics in exchange for scheduled payoffs.

The boys were hyped. This was the big time. As Blake spoke, they displayed their enthusiasm. He continued to whet their appetites and, finally, told them, "Boys, you are dealing with strict taskmasters who tolerate no nonsense. As long as you keep your end of it, you'll be okay. Make no mistakes. The penalties are high."

Diego spoke up. "No problem, man. We run a clean business." The boys laughed and high-fived each other. Diego continued, "We're going to lay low for a couple of weeks . . . you know that creep I shot was a crack head . . . owed us a lot of money, wouldn't pay up." He shrugged and grimaced. "Don't think anyone will miss him."

For a brief moment, Blake couldn't help wondering if somewhere parents were looking for a son. The moment faded as he turned back to his new 'clients'. "I'll be set up soon. Get in touch when you can." Blake reached into his pocket. "Here's a little something for your relaxation." He gave them each a small packet of fine blow.

The boys peeked out at the street and then quickly left, disappearing among the throng of lost souls and the merchants of evil.

Apparently, the coroner's office had done its work. There was no sign of a body or any indication that a shooting had taken place. Blake locked up, jumped into his car and headed back to the hotel.

As he washed and prepared to dress for the evening, he spoke to his image in the mirror. "Well, old boy, it's been a busy day. Time to get ready for Donna; time for some fun." He couldn't get over his luck, hitting pay dirt so fast with the two gang members. The Baron's going to love it.

*   *   *

He arrived at Ivy's bar a few minutes before six. Blake wanted to watch Donna's approach when she entered so he could make an appraisal. He wondered if she would look as good the second time around. With drink in hand, he sat slightly turned on one of the bar stools facing the doorway. Within minutes, she appeared, looking like a movie star. Blake was flabbergasted. She looked even better than he had anticipated. What a knockout! This really was his lucky day. He stood to greet her and kissed her lightly on the cheek.

"Good evening, Mr. Ferguson."

"A pleasure, Donna. Please call me Sean. Now what would you like to drink." He helped her to a bar stool.

"A cosmopolitan would be nice, thank you."

Blake ordered their drinks and was his charming best. He asked a lot of questions and Donna was happy to talk about her past: grew up in Nebraska . . . aspired to be an actress . . . finally, settled for a job as a realtor.

As she spoke, Blake had déjà vu. He couldn't help thinking about Christine. Almost the same story line. For a moment, a shadow crossed his face—a look that worried Donna. Did she say something to upset him? "Oh, Sean, I must be boring you with my tale of woe. Let's have another drink and a fun evening."

"That's fine with me. You're not boring me, Darlin'. I just want this evening to be enjoyable for you," the ever gallant Blake answered.

Donna smiled demurely. "Everything is lovely, Sean. I'm having a great time."

"Where would you like to have dinner?"

"Why don't you choose. Surprise me."

Blake thought for a minute. "How about Ciro's? Food's good and the place is always filled with movie people. You'll enjoy it."

"Sounds wonderful."

They finished their drinks and Blake took care of the tab. As they left, arm in arm, Blake suggested she leave her car and take his to the restaurant. Donna usually went everywhere in her own car, even on dates, but somehow she felt comfortable enough to do as Blake suggested.

When they arrived at Ciro's, Blake spoke with the maitre d' and they were shown to a table, centrally located. "You'll be able to see who's who with no trouble. Now, how about some champagne before we order?"

"Sounds wonderful." Donna was overwhelmed. Sean was incredible . . . and such a gentleman. She felt she was entering a new phase of her life. Somehow, this man might be the answer to her prayers.

The champagne arrived, the waiter poured, and Sean toasted, "Here's to Donna, a beautiful and impressive woman."

She blushed and returned the compliment. "And to Sean, a fine gentleman and wonderful escort. Thank you."

They clinked glasses and then perused the menu while they drank their champagne. Blake asked, "See anything you like? Order whatever your heart desires. Don't be bashful."

Donna was torn between the rack of lamb and the filet mignon. "I'll go with the filet and a baked potato," she finally decided. "No appetizer, though. Fills me up."

"That sounds good to me. I'll have the same. But, after that, you get to choose one of their fabulous desserts which we'll top off with a Cappuccino. How does that sound?"

"Just fantastic. I'm going to enjoy every bit of it."

Blake felt like he had a winner. How lucky can you get? The day's events had been most satisfactory and the evening was even more promising. As they dined, Blake encouraged her to talk about herself and her business, her likes and dislikes, and her pastimes.

Donna felt at ease with him.

From time to time, Blake reached across the table and took her hand in his. "I can't tell you how lucky I feel to have met you, Donna."

"Sean, I'm so happy we met. We're going to be great friends."

"Better friends than you think." He gazed at her intently.

Donna felt a bit flustered. She giggled softly. For a brief moment, she thought she detected a devilish glint in his eyes. His smug expression was somewhat disconcerting. Picky, picky, she told herself, and dismissed any doubts.

Blake sensed some apprehension on her part and sought, immediately, to put it to rest. "Donna, I think you are a terrific gal and I hope we will enjoy a good business relationship. In fact, I need you to find an apartment for me when I return."

"Oh, are you leaving town?"

"Yes, tomorrow. I have some unfinished business to attend to."

"When will you be back and what size apartment did you have in mind, and where?" She had rattled off the question, surprising herself at how flustered she felt.

"I think a two-bedroom and all the rest would suit me fine. When I get back, we'll have dinner to discuss any prospects you come up with. How's that?"

"Oh, okay. Just give me a jingle any morning and we'll make plans. Meanwhile, I'll check the market."

"That's my girl. I knew I had a winner in you."

Donna wished he could see her in a different light. She had to admit, she was extremely attracted to him. However, it seems he's only interested as a client.

"How about that nightcap and cappuccino," he suggested.

Donna nodded in agreement. Blake signaled the waiter.

When they drove back to her car, he said, "Donna, I've really had a great time tonight. I hope you did, too."

"It was just wonderful, Sean."

He helped her into her car and kissed her lightly on the cheek as he said Goodnight. For Donna, this was more disappointing than she wished to admit.

For Blake, it was almost a painful experience. But, he loved to keep his women on the edge.

When he arrived back at his hotel, he used his cell phone to call the Baron's special number. They made small talk until Blake remarked, "I'm meeting friends for lunch tomorrow." That meant he would be arriving at the airport in Mexico at noon.

"Enjoy your lunch and give my regards to Ed."—code for Eduardo will be picking him up.

Conversation ended, Blake called the concierge and asked to be booked on a flight to Mexico City International, arrival time noon the next day. He then showered, got into a comfortable robe and sat in one of the plush armchairs to review his accomplishments, thus far. He was smiling like a Cheshire cat as he nodded off into a deep sleep.

* * *

When Blake told the Baron about the warehouse and of his proposed deals with the Krypton gang members, he greeted the news with enthusiasm. "You did well, my boy. I knew you—what is the expression?—had the right stuff." He gave Blake a bear hug and poured a couple of drinks. "To celebrate our new enterprise. Cheers." Then he added, soberly, "We have a lot to talk about. Remember, I told you it all works point by point."

"Yes, Baron, I remember."

"So, we will carefully lay out a procedure to be followed in the strictest sense . . . every step, every decision well thought out or it could prove to be costly, not only in product but in lives, as well. You understand?"

"Perfectly, Baron. You have my word and my pledge that protocol will be strictly adhered to.

The Baron smiled. "I admire your ability to use appropriate words for the occasion. Well said, my friend."

CHAPTER SEVENTEEN

At the Paramount lot, Christine and Charles were back to routine, shooting her new film, DESIRE. With the exception of a few glitches, production moved along at a steady pace. Christine was thrilled playing opposite Russ again and, now, with Johnny Drew in the cast . . ."Charlie, my cup runneth over," she would say, again and again.

Almost forgotten were the uneasy memories of Blake's unwelcome presence. Christine never spoke of him, but he still lingered in Charles' mind. He only mentioned Blake during his meetings with Jim. "It's like he fell off the edge of the world," Charles said one night.

"Maybe he's got a job elsewhere . . . like Mexico. Remember the talk about him being seen there? If that's so, let's hope he stays there. He's nothing but a pain in the butt." Jim took another gulp of his beer and licked his lips.

"You got that right." Charles turned to the bartender. "Once more with feeling, Tim."

Tim laughed as he put down two newly opened bottles of beer. He got a kick out of the way movie people spoke. As he turned to wash some glasses, Charles stopped him. "See anybody interesting lately?"

"Nah, same old, same old." Then Tim paused. "Saw one new customer the other night . . . thought he looked familiar . . . couldn't place him, though."

Charles perked up. "What made you think you'd seen him before?"

"I dunno. Something about his looks . . . I dunno."

Charles persisted. "What kind of looks? Was he short, tall? Hair? Come on, Tim . . ."

The bartender attempted to draw a more precise description. "About 6'1", short black hair, big mustache . . . good looking guy but not friendly at all." At that moment, he was interrupted by a call for service at the other end of the bar. As he walked away, Charles and Jim exchanged glances. Could it be?

At home, later that night, Charles decided not to mention the conversation at the Pub. Why give Christine something to worry about. The dude probably wasn't Blake anyway.

Charles had a restless night. When he awoke in the morning, Christine was already dressed and had a pot of coffee brewing.

"Come on, lazy bones, have your Java and let's get to the studio for that early call."

Charles studied her as he drank down his coffee. She was so happy with her work and their life together. He was glad he hadn't brought up his conversation with Tim. He hastily drained his cup. "Be ready in a jiff, Honey. Guess I overslept a bit. Blame it on Jimbo. He sure can talk the night away. But, I love the guy."

"He's a great fellow. I'm so glad you have each other's friendship. That's a hard thing to find in this town."

Within a few minutes, they were on their way. As they approached the guard gate at Paramount, Christine said, suddenly, "Charlie, when we get home tonight, I need to have a talk with you about something special."

Perplexed, Charles thought, What in the world? She usually didn't preface any discussion with an early warning. "Sure, Chris . . ." What's on that beautiful mind, he wondered, as he watched her hasten to makeup and wardrobe.

After discussion with Mr. V. regarding new angles, the camera crew was ready to roll. The cast assembled; Mr. V. called, "Lights, Camera, Action!" and another day in the world of make believe began. A ravishing Christine O'Hara faced handsome Russ Crowell, while Johnny Drew played the dastardly villain, lurking in the shadows.

Mr. V.'s new tricks involved a split screen and some sound track innovations. After many takes and retakes, the director finally yelled, "It's a wrap, print it." These are the most welcome words on any set. Actors are, by nature, a superstitious lot. Every time Mr. V. was happy with the dailies, he would gush about what "a big hit" they had on their hands. The actors would make a silent wish, in spite of the tremendous faith they had in his direction. He knew how to work with the camera and the sound system in order to direct the cast to go beyond script pages. Everyone admired his great imagination and daring.

After the day's shooting, Mr. V. announced: "Eight a.m. tomorrow everyone." He sat down on his name inscribed deck chair, blue prints in hand. For him, the work day had not ended. He had some ideas about the next day's shooting—about making his characters come alive—always the consummate director.

Christine and Charles were the last to say goodnight but not before Charles suggested, "Mr. V., it's six o'clock. How about grabbing a quick dinner with us?" The old director looked worn out. Charles looked at Christine for confirmation.

"Oh, yes, please Mr. V.," she graciously added.

"Thanks, kids, but I am determined to block out tomorrow's shoot. Then I'm off to supper with the producers at eight p.m."

"Well, perhaps another time. Enjoy your night." Charles put his arm around Christine.

As he watched them leave, a smile of contentment lit up the director's tired face. Those two are enough to renew my faith in the denizens of this crazy town.

Driving home, Charles waited for Christine to speak. She seemed introspective. "It all went well today, you think? I was worried about the confrontation scene with Johnny Drew."

"It was super. You were fab and so was Drew. Apparently, Mr. V. agreed."

Christine sighed deeply. "I still get butterflies. Still insecure, I guess. Let's see how he feels after he views the dailies."

"Chris, you always look cool and confident, even if you don't feel that way. Butterflies—that's an actor thing."

"Thanks, I really needed that." She leaned over to kiss him.

When they pulled into their driveway, she still hadn't addressed the 'something special' she had mentioned that morning.

Once inside, she said, "I'm going to get out of these duds and hop into a shower. Why don't you do the same?"

"Good idea. You go first and I'll make us a delicious drink."

"No, no, no, Silly. I mean, join me. Got to conserve water, you know." She smiled seductively and hummed a tune from <u>Gypsy</u> as she began disrobing.

Charles followed suit and, within minutes, they were soaping their bodies under the soothing flow of the showerhead. After a sufficient amount of time for love play, Christine said, "Charles I have an idea I'd like to run past you. Let's dry off and get into something comfy."

On the couch, cozy in their terry cloth robes, she turned to him with a serious look on her face. "Darling, we've been living together for over a year and I've loved every minute."

"Me, too, Sweetheart." Where was this going?

"Well, I think it's time I changed my name to Mrs. Charles Markham."

If he weren't in her arms, he would have fallen over. He kissed her emphatically on the lips. "I thought you'd never ask."

"Is that a yes?"

"It's an absolutely. I love you." His voice was hoarse with emotion. "Now, let's have that drink."

They toasted to Mr. and Mrs. Charles Markham, forever and ever. They were lost in the euphoria of the moment until he suggested, "Mrs. Markham, what say we finish this celebration in bed?"

"You betcha!" earned her the usual playful swat on the ass.

*   *   *

They were up early and ready for the eight a.m. studio call. "When we get home this evening, Charlie, I'll tell you what I have in mind for our nuptials." She hugged him.

"I can't wait. We really didn't get to talk much last night." The color rose in his face as he recalled their night of passion.

"You're going to love my idea."

"Any idea of yours is an idea of mine," he quipped.

"Corny!"

"But, true."

They arrived at Paramount and proceeded to Stage 4. The cast was assembled at eight a.m. sharp and the crew was ready to go after the usual preliminaries of make up and instructions from Mr. V.

Charles loved the challenge of the new camera angles and was anxious to test them. He was a student of the Orson Welles' school of innovative filming. He never tired of watching Citizen Kane for its incredible photography. It was a pleasure working with Mr. V. because of his willingness to go the extra mile.

The day's shooting had its highs and lows. Some of the new camera angles didn't work out as Mr. V. had hoped. Charles tried to assuage his frustration. "Not to worry, Mr. V., I believe I can remedy the rough spots. Just need to rethink some of the shots."

"Charles, you are the only cinematographer I know who's got the guts to humor a maverick like me."

"Your body of work speaks for itself. I don't know anyone who doesn't regard it an honor to work with you."

"Thanks, Charles." Mr. V. reflected on how fond he was of Charles. He then turned to issue instructions. "Eight a.m. for the cast tomorrow.

Camera crew on set at seven. We've got work to do. Okay with you, Charles?

"Fine, Mr. V."

*   *   *

Once again in their car, Christine became animated. "Charlie, what do you think of this? We ask Mr. V. if we can get married at his beach house in Malibu. We can have the ceremony down by the water's edge and a lovely buffet inside and . . ."

"Whoa! Sounds great but that's a big favor to ask."

"I know, but wouldn't it be a beautiful thing . . . and so romantic. Besides, I know Mr. V. loves us. Let's ask him. I'm so excited." Her eyes glistened.

Charles reached for her hand. "Sweetheart, I'll talk to Mr. V. I know how much he loves you . . . like the daughter he never had. Told me so himself."

"Thanks, Charlie. I can hardly wait. I'll call my mom and dad and tell them to prepare for a Hollywood wedding. They'll be so happy."

"Guess I'll do the same. I feel guilty about not seeing my folks these last few years. They're going to be happy to hear that I'm giving up my bachelorhood."

"But, Charlie, they know we've been living together this past year . . ."

"Yes, but with their old fashioned ideas, 'living together' is a Hollywood thing, not the real thing."

She smiled. "It's been more than real for me."

He kissed her on the forehead and guided the car into the garage. They decided to have a light meal of tuna sandwiches, Cape Cod potato chips and iced tea. Her enthusiasm did not diminish as she kept up a constant chatter about their forthcoming wedding. Charles sat quietly listening and observing how positively enticing she was.

After a while, he took her by the hand. "And so to bed."

CHAPTER EIGHTEEN

The past week at the Baron's had been boring for Blake, except for the plans for distributing the cocaine, marijuana, and methamphetamine. Enormous profits never ceased to interest him. With Rosa out of town on a gig, he was not a happy camper. Even though there were lots of attractive women around, he knew better than to play the field at the Baron's. Rosa's temper was as explosive as her talent. Whether she was acting, singing, or dancing she had the ability to electrify her audience. Her wrath at any infidelity on Blake's part would be no less effective. He comforted himself with the thought that there would be better nights back in L.A.

When he returned, he checked in at the Orlando Hotel which was centrally located on West 3rd Street and a short ride to Sunset Strip. He liked the proximity. As soon as he unpacked, he put a call through to Donna. "Hi, Gorgeous, guess who's back in town."

"Sean, it's you!" Her breath caught in her throat. She tried to be nonchalant but her heart was racing. "Glad to hear from you again. Have a good trip?"

"Yes. Did you miss me?"

"Sure and I've been doing my homework. I think I've found some good prospects for you . . ."

"Is that all you can talk about—business?" he teased. "I want to know if you missed me."

There he goes again with that personal touch, Donna thought. "Of course, I missed you. I always miss my friends when they are away."

Blake, who was a master at the game, broke into friendly laughter. "You're such an adorable friend, Donna. Come on, tell me how much you missed me or I won't go to see any apartments with you," he said, playfully.

She was the one to laugh this time. "Okay. Yes, I did miss you. We had such fun that night before you left." Donna stopped talking. She was afraid she might show exactly how she felt, how much her mind had dwelled upon him all week.

"Okay, then it's time to have some more fun. How about dinner tonight?"

"Great," a happy Donna replied. "I'd love it . . . and I can tell you all about the apartments I found for you."

At that moment, Blake's priorities were channeling in a different direction. Her repeated references to apartments annoyed him, but again, he teased, "I'm beginning to think that's all you really care about, but I'll take you to dinner anyway. So, Sweetie, how's about six o'clock, same bar, same place. I'm a sentimental guy."

"Sounds good to me." Was he telling her that their date meant something to him? "See you at six." She hung up quickly, closed her eyes and sighed softly.

*   *   *

After his conversation with Donna, Blake changed his attire, arranged for a rental and headed to the warehouse. The Baron had advised him to expect shipment of stock within three days—the exact day and time of delivery would be disclosed on his cell phone.

Blake got down to business at once. He checked out sign makers and painters, got estimates and scheduled the work. He located an office furniture store and arranged for a desk and chair, a file cabinet, two armchairs, lamps and accessories to be delivered later in the week. In the interim, he would have a cleaning crew come in to scrub down the place.

He was beaming with satisfaction by the time he returned to his hotel. "And just think," he said aloud, "an evening with a lovely damsel is yet to come." Blake had every intention of making sure that his evening with Donna would complete what he considered to be a most satisfactory day.

In the shower, he sang excerpts from <u>South Pacific</u> in an exuberant voice . . ."some enchanted evening" . . . like a man without a care in the world.

Six o'clock sharp, Blake and Donna warmly greeted each other and sat perched on bar stools at Ivy's enjoying their Cosmopolitans. "Tonight, Beautiful, we are going to dine in one of the best seafood restaurants in L.A. Do you like lobster?"

"Love it . . . when I can afford it."

"Well, be my guest and enjoy to your heart's content."

"You're so sweet, Sean. No one's ever treated me so well. I feel like Cinderella."

"And I feel like the prince." He kissed her hand.

Now on her second Cosmo, Donna had a good feeling about the way things were going. She felt giddy.

Blake suggested, "One more cocktail and we're off to the Gulfstream on Monica Boulevard. You're going to love the lobster."

By the time they got to Blake's car, Donna was feeling no pain. "Wow, pardon the French, but those drinks were enough to knock me on my tush." She giggled sheepishly.

Blake hugged her and helped her into his car. "We'll come back for yours later."

"Sounds good to me." Donna was more than willing.

The popular restaurant was brimming over with clientele. All the tables were taken except for the one Blake had reserved. He ordered a fine white wine and a pound and a half lobster for each of them, with appropriate sides. The waiter provided the bibs and the dismantling began.

"I always feel guilty tearing these poor creatures apart," Donna said.

"But they are so delicious and worth the trouble, aren't they?"

"Yes, but I can't help being a little sad about it."

Blake smiled at her. "Well, then you should be sad about almost anything you eat, you know, like steak, lamb chops . . ."

Donna cut in. "Point taken but it doesn't alter my feelings."

Blake was about to change the subject when he heard a familiar voice he did not wish to acknowledge.

"Excuse me, but aren't you Blake Dugan?" It was one of the extras from THE FLAWLESS MISTRESS. "I think we worked in a movie together . . ."

"You're making a mistake."

The intruder persisted. "Weren't you in . . ."

Blake's angry voice cut him off. "You're disturbing our dinner."

"Gosh, I'm sorry. I just thought . . ."

"Get lost, Buster." Blake averted his face. It was dark with emotion.

The sharpness of his retorts was not lost on Donna. If she had been totally sober, she would have questioned it. Now, it was a fleeting thought as she gulped down her wine and turned her attention to the nut cracker as it did its work.

For the next few minutes, Blake brooded, making little conversation. So, my cover's not as good as I thought. That could prove to be a problem.

Donna continued to eat quietly, sensing his irritability. Mistakes happen, she thought. Why did he get so bent out of shape? She shrugged and continued to finish what remained of the lobster.

"Sean, I can't tell you how much I am enjoying this meal," she told him as she mouthed her last bite. I'm just sorry that you got so upset . . ." She hesitated.

"I'm not upset, Darlin'. I just hate to be interrupted when I'm dining with a beautiful woman." He took her hand in his and kissed it, as he morphed into his charming self.

Donna felt a tingle. He sure knows how to romance a girl. "I understand," but she really did not. "Sean, everything is so perfect."

"You're perfect," he said, looking deeply into her eyes.

Donna smiled. He's back.

The rest of the evening went well. Soon they were on their way to pick up her car.

Blake suggested, "I have a great idea. It's not that late. Why don't we have a nightcap at my place?"

A giddy Donna asked, "Are you trying to seduce me, Sir?"

He pulled her roughly to him and kissed her hard on the mouth. "If I am, do I hear a vote of confidence?"

She answered huskily, "Yes, Sean, yes."

They stopped at Ivy's to pick up her car and she followed him to the Orlando. Donna was gradually accepting what Blake took for granted: she would be spending the night.

When she awoke in his bed the next morning, she reviewed the events of the night. For some reason, while she remembered the enjoyable moments, Sean's angry face kept intruding. Now sober, it gave her pause.

He interrupted her thoughts with a bear hug. "We had a wonderful evening . . . and night . . . but now it's time for breakfast and then to work."

"Yes, it was wonderful." She kissed him. "I've got to pass on breakfast. Got to get home and change before I report to the office. I'll call you later. Maybe we can look at a couple of rentals . . ."

"I don't know about today. I'll call you." With deliveries expected, Blake did not want to make a commitment. He couldn't afford to screw up, but he definitely wanted to keep Donna 'on hold'.

He took her to her car in the parking lot and then picked his car up from the garage. He decided to go to the warehouse before catching a bite to eat. When he got there, the place was a beehive of activity. The painters were working outside. The cleaning crew, inside. Tomorrow, the furniture will arrive and his sign would be up on the building by the end of the week.

He drove over to a small, nearby café and had brunch. He returned to the warehouse where he sat in his car out front to watch as the work progressed. He felt quite impressed with himself. Suddenly, his cell phone rang.

"Hello. TV Parts and Specialties?" a familiar voice asked.

"Yes, it is." Blake answered the Baron's question.

"Our truck will be delivering the items you ordered tomorrow afternoon, between three and five o'clock."

"Confirmed. Thank you." Blake waited but there was only a click at the other end. The Baron's playing it safe. Don't blame him. This is new territory, with a new cast of characters.

By mid-afternoon, Blake decided to place a call to Donna's office. He was told by the realtor on floor duty that Donna was out with a client. "May I take a message?"

"Yes. Tell her Sean Ferguson will meet her at the same place, same time, tonight." His self-assurance was on a high.

The realtor disliked messages of this kind. Had Donna expected this call? "Is there a number at which you can be reached, if it's not convenient for her?"

Blake was miffed. "Donna has my number. Just make sure she gets my message."

The realtor was annoyed by the arrogance in the caller's voice, however, she assured him his message would be relayed.

He hung up abruptly and turned his attention to the painters. They looked like they would be finishing shortly. He glanced at his wristwatch . . . three thirty. If I can make it back to my hotel by four thirty, it'll give me plenty of time to get ready and be at Ivy's by six.

*   *   *

Still sitting alone at Ivy's bar at six thirty, Blake became irritated. When he called Donna's apartment, there was no answer—only the tape. By seven, he was in a black mood. Several drinks did not assuage it. Did that bitch in the office give Donna his message?

The bartender grew apprehensive as he watched Blake get more surly with each drink. What Ivy's didn't need was trouble. "Sir, may I get you a cup of coffee, perhaps? Take the edge off . . . ?"

"Mind your own business. If I want coffee, I know where to get it. Now, pour me another scotch and soda and get lost."

The maitre d' was alerted by Blake's loud words. His next move was on a signal from the bartender. He approached Blake and said quietly, but firmly, "I'm sorry, Sir, but I will have to ask you to leave. We cannot serve you anymore. This request is for your benefit as well as ours."

Blake was furious but had the presence of mind to realize he was bringing unwanted attention to himself. He grumbled something about the check, removed a $100 dollar bill from his wallet and slammed it down on the bar before storming out.

The saying that God watches over drunks held true for Blake. He drove erratically back to the Orlando, valet parked, and stumbled from the elevator to his room. After he undressed and had a cold shower, he made a call to Donna's apartment. Still no answer. He was in a miserable mood as he poured himself a drink and plunked down on the couch. It was fortunate that he soon fell fast asleep . . . but not so fortunate that he did not hear Donna's ring.

In the morning, he awoke with a roaring headache. As he brooded over his room service breakfast, the phone rang.

"Sean, what's wrong?" It was Donna. "I expected to hear from you yesterday."

"Don't give me that 'what's wrong' crap. I called your office and left a message for you to meet me at Ivy's."

"Oh, Sean, I'm so sorry. I was out with clients all day and never went back to my office. Why didn't you call my cell phone? When I got back to my apartment at night, I did call you but there was no answer. I didn't know you had called during the day. Please don't be angry. It's just a mistake."

"Don't they forward messages to your cell or home phone?" His anger was mounting. "You bet I'm angry."

"Pu-leeze, do I get a second chance?" she cajoled.

Blake did not want to spoil this promising relationship, so he controlled himself. "Okay, Baby, you got it. Listen, I'm heading out to the warehouse. Call me at three o'clock and we'll make plans. How's that grab you?"

"In all the right places, Honey." She laughed. "Talk to you at three. 'Bye." When she clicked off, she had mixed emotions. Desire, tinged with an inexplicable apprehension. Again, he had displayed a cold, hard side. "Well," she told herself, "we'll just have to soften him up, won't we?"

*   *   *

Back on Central and 6th, things were moving right along. The painting was completed. The furniture arrived, as promised, and by mid-afternoon, Blake was awaiting the arrival of his supplies. At three o'clock sharp, Donna called. "Hi, Hon, how's your day going?"

Blake, who was still a little peeved about the night before, decided to give her a hard time. "Donna, I'm having a busy day so far and expect to be tied up into the evening. Why don't we plan on tomorrow. I'll call you."

Disappointed, Donna responded, "Oh, sure, if you're busy . . ."

"Yes, I am. Talk to you in the a.m." Blake enjoyed the regret in her voice. Tough.

At four thirty p.m., a large delivery van pulled into the driveway. The driver jumped out and identified himself and the supplies he was delivering. Blake directed the driver to pull into the bay of the warehouse. Code words and money were exchanged. Boxes of TV parts and supplies were unloaded. One carton was marked Fragile, and set aside from the rest. The driver advised Blake, "You will be particularly careful with this one." He gave Blake a knowing look and was on his way.

The necessary call was put through to the Baron who was happy to hear that everything was on schedule. In couched terms, he gave Blake further instructions regarding the distribution of the contents in the carton marked Fragile. "For the present, you will do business with local gangs. Use extreme caution regarding payments for merchandise. All cash, up front. Trust no one."

"Of course. You know how I am."

The usual click at the other end.

Just then who should suddenly make an appearance but Diego and Alex. "Hey, man, how's it going'?" Alex extended a handshake, while Diego mumbled a greeting.

"Well, well," Blake said, "the return of the natives."

"Huh?" Diego muttered.

Blake looked them over. Was he really going to deal with these creeps? They'd better have the money, or it's *adios muchachos*. "Well, welcome back, guys. Have a good vacation? Ready to get down to business?"

"Yeah, we had a swell time. And we are more than ready to do business. That's why we're here. What have you got for us?"

"Nothing tonight. Come back in the morning. I'll have it all sorted out for you. Tell me what you need."

Diego was adamant. "We gotta do some business tonight. Got a couple of interested dudes who can't wait."

Blake decided it was not a good idea to turn them away but he needed to stall for time so he could open the 'fragile' carton. "Tell you what, I've got to get some food under my belt. I'm meeting a business contact at a restaurant nearby. I can't cancel on him. Why don't you boys go out and have a meal, on me." He handed them two $20 dollar bills.

"Cool." Alex grabbed the money. "Be back in a couple."

"With cash," Blake emphasized.

He closed the warehouse, got into his car and watched as the boys drove away. When they were out of sight, he opened the bay door, pulled his car in and lowered the door behind him. He immediately went to work. In the carton was an ample supply of cocaine—more than enough for a test run. He knew what he had to get for the stuff. "I hope those clowns come up with enough dough," he said, as he picked up several plastic bags of cocaine, checking the grams and calculating the price. He had hoped to delay starting any business until after his crew—his backup—arrived. They weren't due until tomorrow. However, he didn't want to back off on the Kryptons tonight. And, just in case, he retrieved his hand gun from the glove compartment of his car.

In less than two hours, the boys returned. Their eyes widened when Blake offered them cocaine at a price they had anticipated would be much higher.

"Your price is good, but if the coke isn't . . ." Alex shrugged.

Blake said, "Pick any bag you like, open it and check it out. I guarantee you, this is the best you'll ever get."

Alex did the honors, and acknowledged, "Good deal." A wad of $100 dollar bills were extracted from his pocket. He shelled out the requested amount and placed the packages of cocaine in his backpack.

Blake, satisfied with the transaction, said, "It's been a pleasure, gentlemen. Call this number when you need to order." He handed them a slip of paper which read, "Private Mr. F. The number on it was in Blake's private collection.

After they left, Blake thought about what a great beginning it was. This deserves a celebration. He locked up, put the top down on his convertible and headed for the Strip. He didn't want to waste his good mood. He was tempted to call Donna but quickly changed his macho mind. The Strip would be fun. No problem finding companionship, if he wanted it. Variety is the spice of life.

Blake laughed out loud and the wind carried the sounds far into the night.

CHAPTER NINETEEN

The next morning, Blake called room service and ordered breakfast and a copy of the L.A. Times. He was in a great mood. Last night, bar hopping and enjoying the scene on the Strip was fun. He hadn't lacked for female companionship. Now, he decided, he would call Donna when he finished eating to set up a date for the evening.

As he browsed through the newspaper, he ate with gusto. Suddenly, an article jumped out at him.

"Leading lady Christine O'Hara and cinematographer Charles Markham, in an interview last night on 'What's New in Hollywood', announced that they had set their wedding date. They have been an item since they met two years ago and it has proven to be an excellent collaboration, both personally and professionally.

"The nuptials will take place on June 20th, 1998, seaside in Malibu, at the home of Director John Victor, who directed Ms. O'Hara's first film, THE FLAWLESS MISTRESS, and is currently working with her on DESIRE.

"A buffet reception, indoors, will follow a seaside ceremony, weather permitting. In attendance will be family members and close friends from the movie community."

Blake nearly choked on the toast he was ingesting. He gulped down a mouthful of coffee. "Damn!" he shouted. A stream of expletives followed. "We'll see about that. I'm not through with you yet, Christine." He'd been so preoccupied lately, he'd hardly thought about her. Occasionally, his mind had wandered in her direction, but he had put everything on hold until he could expedite his plan. Now this wedding business put a whole new face on things.

He hurriedly dressed, called for his car and hastened down to the warehouse. He realized he hadn't called Donna but shelved the idea for later. There was work to be done. Shortly, after he arrived and was arranging the furniture in his office, three men reported for work. So, this was his backup, Blake mused, as he assessed them. Only one looked like he could hold his own.

The man spoke first. "I am Manuel and this is Tony and Alfredo. Mr. Sony sent us." (Sony being the operative word.)

The Baron had assured Blake they were trustworthy and capable.

"Welcome, my friends. You come highly recommended. We'll do well together. Do you have accommodations?"

"Yes, the Baron has arranged everything," Manuel answered. The other two nodded in agreement.

Blake immediately put them to task, arranging and stacking the TV items in their cartons, leaving one sample each on display. From the invoice supplied by the driver, prices were determined and products tagged.

"Tomorrow we have some work to do on the office wall behind my desk . . . a *caleta,* understand? . . . a hiding place. Now take a break for lunch and we'll finish the tags later."

The three men left. Blake dialed Donna's office number.

"Good afternoon, Donna Golden speaking. How may . . ."

Blake cut her off. "Donna, I'm up to my eyeballs here, but how about I pick you up at seven tonight? Give me the address . . ."

"I can meet you, if that's more convenient."

Blake, who was still not fully recovered from his black mood of the morning, yelled, "Are you paying attention? I said I'd pick you up! Give me the damn address!"

Donna was speechless. There's that temper again. She hesitated and then, almost in a whisper, she answered, "I'm at the Bunker Hill Towers, 234 S. Figureron Street, Apt. 2A. I'll be ready at seven. Have the doorman ring me."

"Fine. See you then." Blake hung up.

Donna stood silently for a moment. One of her colleagues approached her. She was concerned by the look on Donna's face. "Anything wrong, Donna? You look upset."

"No, no, Addy. I'm all right. Just thinking about something."

"Or, someone, I'd say, and not happy thoughts at that."

A phone call interrupted their conversation. Addy backed off.

*   *   *

When Blake's men returned from their lunch, they finished tagging and awaited further instructions. It was still early, so Blake explained what he wanted with reference to the hiding place in his office.

"It shouldn't take more than a day or so," Manuel assured him. He then left with his men in their pick up truck to get the necessary supplies. While they were gone, Blake made sure that the Krypton's money was secure.

The three men returned with panels of plywood and other necessities. Blake was pleased. "Good show. You're really on the ball."

Blake felt satisfied that the whole operation would be a snap and the rewards plentiful. It was all falling into place. The Baron had promised him he would be a wealthy man. Well, he was on his way. By six o'clock, he called it a day and sent the men off to their own resources. Back at the Orlando, he stood in front of his bathroom mirror, shaving and singing, "I believe in you . . ." Self-confidence was one virtue he did possess.

Promptly at seven, the doorman called Donna's apartment. "Mr. Ferguson is on his way up."

When she opened the door, she greeted him warmly. He just stared at her. *This broad looks better every time I see her.* "Hi, Gorgeous, want to have dinner with a lonely guy?"

Her kiss was her response.

"Hey, one more of those and dinner is canceled," he joked.

"Nu-uh! This is one hungry gal here."

"Dinner it is, then . . . but the night is young." Blake kept his arm around her waist as he escorted her to his car.

Donna was relieved that he was in good spirits.

He took her to the Beverly Wilshire Hotel in Beverly Hills where they dined in a romantic setting on the patio. Donna couldn't help but be impressed. *He sure knows how to wine and dine a girl.*

The evening culminated in exciting hours of love making in her bed. Before he left, he promised to see her the next day to do his apartment hunting. Donna was one happy girl as the door closed behind Blake. *Things were progressing . . .*

As he drove back to his hotel, streaks of grey and yellow colored the dawn of a new day. He was in high gear emotionally, having just spent a 'fabulous night with a fabulous woman.' Blake checked his wristwatch. *There's still time to catch an hour or so in the sack.*

Back in his room, he did exactly that.

*   *   *

He was a little late in arriving at the warehouse the next morning. The three men were there waiting for him. "Sorry, but I had a busy night." He winked at them. His reputation with the ladies preceded him; the men laughed and gave him a thumb's up.

Blake called Donna, arranged to take her to lunch at Izzy's Deli and then to go apartment hunting. To save time, Donna said she would pick him up at the warehouse. When they were in her car, Blake told her. "You'll love Izzy's—it's the deli to the stars. Never know who might be having a corned beef sandwich or a couple of dogs near you."

"I've always wanted to go there."

"Anything your heart desires, Donna."

She smiled at him.

They had a fun lunch while they went over the list she had compiled of possibilities. Blake was interested in location so he opted to check out the Crescent at W. Hollywood on No. Crescent Heights Boulevard and the Town Center Apartments on Andover Drive. He wasn't sold on either one. "What about the Beverly Hills Towers where you rent? Your place is right in the middle of everything. I like that."

Donna hesitated. She hadn't suggested it because she wasn't sure about having him take up residence in such close proximity. As much as she was enamored of him, she still harbored doubts about his erratic and, at times, dominating behavior. "Sean, I don't know what, if anything, is available right now. I'd have to check."

"You don't sound so keen on the idea. What's the matter, Baby, got something else going for you?" His voice had that edge again.

"No, of course not, Honey. I'll check it out when I get back to the office."

His response was a dissatisfied grunt. They drove back to the warehouse in silence. Blake jumped out of her car, saying, "Call you in the morning."

Donna tried hard to hide her disappointment. "Okay. Have a good evening." She drove off.

Blake hastened inside. He was anxious to see how far his crew had gotten with the wall project. The men were busy sawing and hammering. "Looks like you'll be finished tomorrow, eh?" Blake was pleased with their progress.

Manuel answered, "For sure, tomorrow."

Blake stretched out in one of the armchairs. For the first time since breakfast, his thoughts dwelled on the wedding announcement in the newspaper. His mood changed instantly. He cursed out loud. The three men turned toward him. "Anything wrong, Senor Blake?" Manuel asked.

"No, no, nothing. I just remembered something I'm not happy about . . . not to worry, it has nothing to do with you." Blake realized that his blue language had been misinterpreted as a reflection on their work. Got to be more careful. These men are members of the Baron's 'special cadre'.

By six o'clock, Blake suggested, "What do you say we grab a bite to eat at the café down the street? Enough work for today, *amigos.*"

The idea was greeted with gusto.

Blake figured that eating in the neighborhood would give him the opportunity to observe the evening activity on the street. It was time to start broadening his horizons. He had to build up a substantial clientele to keep the Baron happy, not to mention himself.

After they had eaten, Blake told them to separate and circulate around the street. They new the drill. Blake told them, "If you see any gang members dealing, approach carefully and refer them to me, after you explain how it will benefit them. Use caution. I'll sit here and have a drink."

The men knew what to do. They were experienced in this type of operation. They separated and scanned each side of the street. Immediately, Manuel noticed a bag man in a tee shirt bearing the insignia of a skull and cross bones. The name Lords of Vice was clearly imprinted underneath. After a few implicit exchanges, the gang member followed Manuel to the café. To the average person, it could have been a chance meeting. They chatted a while and then Blake set up an appointment with "Brute" to meet later that night in the warehouse.

Tony and Alfredo returned soon after with two casually dressed fellows who Blake spotted as pushers, as he had watched them engage in conversation across the street. They enjoyed a drink together, had a 'meaningful' talk and arranged a meeting for ten in the morning, next day.

Blake complimented his men. "Good work. Now, let's get back to the warehouse." In short order, Brute showed up with another gang member who wore a similar 'deadly' tee shirt who he introduced as, "Chuck, second in command."

Manuel, Tony and Alfredo stationed themselves for quick action, if needed.

Blake invited the two gang members into his office. On his desk were samples of cocaine. They discussed quantities and price after Blake invited them to do a taste test of the fine, powdery substance. They expressed their satisfaction with the product. "Man, that's good blow!" Brute said. "My customers have been complaining lately. They weren't getting the desired results. They'll love this stuff."

Blake told them, "Be here with the cash at eight a.m. tomorrow and I'll have your order ready. They shook hands and left.

Blake's men bid him goodnight. He locked up, got into his convertible and headed back to the Orlando, singing all the way, "What a day this has been . . ."

*   *   *

Promptly at eight, the next morning, Brute appeared with the cash and the deal they had made the night before was completed.

At ten a.m., the two men with whom Blake had spoken the previous night, turned up. Blake made them welcome and invited them into his office. Manuel alerted his men. Within a short time, product and money exchanged hands.

Time to call the Baron. Blake did the usual cell phone thing and was greeted with the usual silence. "Good morning. How's the weather there?" he asked.

"Fine. You should spend a few days." That signaled that the Baron wanted to see him.

"I'm pretty busy right now. Can I visit on the weekend?"

"Yes."

"I'll call when I firm up my plans. Thanks for the invite."

Click.

Blake would have a lot to tell the Baron. Meanwhile, he hoped to rope in at least one more potential client within the next few days. He turned to Manuel. "How about taking a walk. It's a nice day. You might meet someone interesting."

Taking the cue, Manuel said, "Good idea. A little fresh air will be enjoyable and a new friend is always welcome, eh?" He strode out of the warehouse and down the street.

Suddenly, there were sounds of screaming and sirens. Someone had been shot. Another initiation into a gang. A prospective member was given a gun and told to go out and kill a rival gang member.

Manuel, who was no stranger to violence, returned to the warehouse, white-faced. "My God, they are just children . . . this boy just walked up and put a bullet through the other boy's heart."

Blake was surprised at Manuel's reaction. He wondered who the victim was. A client, perhaps? Manuel had said that he was not close enough to identify the killer but he did notice that the shirt of the slain boy had the skull and crossbones on it. One of the Lords of Vice.

A little while later, the phone rang. "This is Chuck. Brute's left town. You'll be dealing with me from now on."

It was obvious who had been at the short end of the bullet. Blake wondered who was at the other end of the gun. Bears looking into. He sent Tony out to reconnoiter. It wasn't too long before Tony returned. "Nobody's talking to nobody. The street's quiet as death. Lots of 'blue' around."

"Figures." Blake said.

*   *   *

That weekend at the Baron's, Blake was given some news. Eduardo had been assigned to set up an operation in San Diego similar to Blake's. "There is much potential and things are happening quickly. Eduardo has been progressing very well," the Baron told him.

Blake was a little bent out of shape over this, but he hid his feelings. He wanted to be the only golden boy. "I'm glad to hear that, Baron. I had no idea you were spreading out."

"Well, you will understand why soon enough . . . and how it works. Remember, always point by point. With Eduardo in San Diego and you in L.A., there is potential for both of you to become transportation coordinators for distribution to cells in cities all over the country. We will talk more about this when Eduardo arrives tonight."

Blake, with free time on his hands until then, went to look for Rosa. She was still on the road. Frustrated, he went to the bar, poured himself a drink and went out to the patio where he stared at the shimmering waters of the placid lake.

Summoning his favorite and only word he knew in French, he growled through clenched teeth, "Merde!" Circumstances, so far, did not bode well for him. It was getting too complicated. The thought crossed his mind that he should never have gotten into this game—a game from which a player never leaves voluntarily.

This was not Blake, the control freak. This was Blake freaking out. For the first time that he could remember, he was apprehensive . . . and that scared him.

CHAPTER TWENTY

The final scenes for DESIRE were action street shots in areas that could be cordoned off. These were completed within a week. Everyone was excited about the rushes.

"It will be another premiere spectacular at Grauman's," Mr. V. predicted. He was pleased that filming had gone without a hitch. Cast and crew had jelled well, he thought, not like the nonsense during MISTRESS with that two-bit actor Blake something-or other. What was his last name anyway. He shrugged, brushing the thought aside.

With the film wrapping up and the nuptials only a few months away, Christine suggested, "Charlie, let's take a break and spend some time alone away from here. I told Mr. V. that we needed a hiatus and he agreed . . . but, he warned that he already had potential properties in mind."

"Well, Chris, in this business you can't afford the luxury of a private life. Time is a fleeting thing."

"Charlie, my time with you is paramount, not Paramount . . ." She stopped and they both laughed at the unintentional play on words.

*　　*　　*

The producers of DESIRE planned a big cast and crew party to be held at the Mocambo on St. Patrick's Day. Besides being fun for all, it was good PR.

"It's always a special time after a project is completed and getting together is fun. And, if anyone should ask, it can't hurt to say we have a sure-fire hit in the can." Mr. V. was beaming.

Christine and Charles had two weeks in which to make their getaway. A gleeful Christine told him she had arranged for their stay at the same villa they had previously rented in Mexico. "We made so many wonderful memories there and now we can make even more."

Charles loved to see her happy. He hugged her close. "Chris, it sounds perfect. We're going to have the time of our lives."

She giggled. "Who would ever suspect you are a movie person?"

*   *   *

It so happened that Blake Dugan was in town March 17th but was not aware of the celebration at the Mocambo. He had just come back into town from a visit with the Baron. True to his Gaelic origins, he loved to raise a pint or two in honor of the man who drove the snakes from Ireland.

He dialed Donna's number. "I'm ba-a-ck! Pick you up at six for dinner and then we're on the town, Baby."

Donna was happy. "Sounds great, Sean. I can hardly wait to see you." She replaced the phone. Things were going well between them. She wasn't able to get him a rental in her complex so Blake had maintained his digs at the Orlando. She didn't question his business trips but often wondered about them. She wondered, too, about the warehouse and the men working there. Once in a while, on her way to meet a client, she had occasion to pass the warehouse. The obvious lack of activity surprised her. No truck deliveries at a time of day when such activity was normal. The bay door was usually closed. It puzzled her but she knew some things were better left unsaid where Sean was concerned.

At promptly six p.m., the doorman buzzed her intercom. "A gentleman awaits you in his Mercedes at the entrance." He enjoyed making his announcements with a little added touch because he knew it made Donna laugh.

"Thanks, Ted." It surprised her that Sean was waiting downstairs. He usually came up for a cocktail or two, "to start the night properly", he would say. It wasn't the drinking she cared about, it was the intimacy—the promise of what was to come.

Checking the mirror for a last minute appraisal, she whispered to her reflection, "There is something to be said for anticipation." She remembered her father's words: "Sweetheart, the anticipation is always more enjoyable than the *fait accompli*." She didn't believe it then, but the ensuing years taught her that Daddy's philosophy was often right on the mark . . . except for Sean. Anticipation with him usually resulted in new, unexpected pleasures. "Wonder what he has in mind tonight?"

When she got into the car, he took her into his arms and kissed her passionately, displaying an urgency she hadn't experienced with him before.

"Well, hello there, Handsome. Where have you been all my life?" She kissed him back.

"Waiting for you, Gorgeous. You look smashing, as the Brits would say. Girl, you get better every time." He pulled her close.

She laughed and asked, "Want to park the car and come upstairs?"

"Yes, but not now. We're going to the Irish Pub, fill ourselves with Irish Stew and wash it all down with tankards of Irish coffee . . . as many as it takes. How does that sound?"

"Like the perfect opening to a grand finale," she replied enthusiastically.

At the Pub, things were humming. Blake felt safe in assuming he wouldn't be recognized. After all, he had passed the test months ago. The waitress showed them to a booth.

"What a quaint watering hole. How did I ever miss this one?"

"Stick with me, Baby." Blake laughed. "Nothing but the best."

The evening was fun. They made jokes about Mulligan stew, Irish wakes, and anything else they could convert into something Irish.

All the while, Tim, behind the bar swamped with celebrants, kept glancing over at them. The laughter erupting from their booth every few minutes attracted his attention. When Donna stood up to go to the ladies' room, Tim noticed that her escort stood up, as well. Quite the gentleman. Tim nudged his assistant and pointed to Donna. "She's a beauty, all right!"

"She sure is," he agreed. "Never seen her in here before. You?"

"Nope." Tim turned his sights on Blake. "But, I swear I've seen him before." He paused. "Know what? That dude came in alone one night . . . I wondered about him . . ." Tim shrugged and turned back to his customers. But, he couldn't help wonder.

"Hello, Tim. How've you been?" a friendly voice asked.

Tim swung around to see Jim Green taking a seat on one of the barstools. A broad smile lit up his face. "Hey, long time no see. How are you and how is Mr. Markham? Hear Christine is in another biggie."

"Yes. Movie's done and the whole company is out celebrating tonight. I'm supposed to meet Charles here for a couple of brews. Said he'd be here after the dinner party, about now. Christine had to beg off. Poor girl, she's exhausted."

Tim smiled. "It'll be good to serve you both again. Miss you guys." He hesitated. "Don't get me wrong; I'm not talking about business. Always liked you two. You're real gentlemen."

"Tim, this place will always be special for us. This is where Charles met Christine, remember?"

"Right." Tim smiled broadly.

Time has a way of manipulating moments, and hence, the actions of people, in an inexplicable way. At the instant that Charles stepped into the Pub, Blake was paying his tab. Then as he led Donna to the back door out to the parking lot, Charles was approaching the restrooms. They passed within a hare's breath of each other, unaware.

When Charles returned to the bar, Tim asked, "Did you happen to notice the guy and beautiful lady just going out the back door?"

"No, why?"

"I dunno. That guy looks familiar. Ya know, now that I think of it, he reminds me of that dope peddler you used to ask me about."

Charles and Jim exchanged glances. Tim had a good eye. Charles jumped up and ran toward the back door. Outside, he observed a couple in a Mercedes convertible, making out like crazy. He was about to turn away when he heard a voice he would never mistake. The hair on his arms bristled as he tried to look more closely, but the brights on the car lit up and the Mercedes, in gear, swerved out to the avenue. Charles cursed aloud, startling some patrons who were just leaving.

Blake, on the other hand, suffered no doubts as to whom he had just seen. Was Christine there in the Pub? Damn!

Back at the bar, Charles was fuming. "I could swear that bastard Blake was behind the wheel."

Jim tried to calm him down by changing the subject, but Charles was relentless.

"The viper has resurfaced. Now what?"

Jim tried to assuage him. "Even if it was Blake with a gorgeous chick . . . looks like he's moved on. No reason to worry about him bothering Christine. Come on, Charlie, let's have another brewsky and head to the diner for coffee."

Charles sensed his friend's frustration and answered apologetically, "I'm sorry to be such a nudge. One more beer and it's coffee time." He smiled weakly.

*   *   *

Back at Donna's apartment, she poured them a nightcap. Before he finished his drink, Blake suddenly jumped up. "I'm sorry, Donna, but

I've got to go. Just remembered something I've got to take care of." He kissed her absent-mindedly and hastened out the door before she could say a word.

Donna was in shock. What had happened in the last few minutes? The anticipated night of pleasure had taken an unexpected turn. Did she do something that displeased him? The night had been so perfect. Reflecting upon her father's philosophy, she said aloud, "Daddy, you sure were right on the button tonight. The anticipation was far more enjoyable."

Blake drove back, at high speed, to the Pub. The old longing had resurfaced. When he saw Charles, he had wondered if Christine was there. He had to know. Entering from the back door, he scanned the booths and the bar. There was still quite a crowd—but no Christine or Charles.

Tim caught a glimpse of Blake as he was turning toward the restrooms. He poked the other bartender. "I'll be damned. There's that guy again. He's like a freakin' phantom. This ain't no public toilet. He'd better buy a drink. I'd like to get a good look at him, anyway."

Blake, although uncertain, sauntered over to the bar. He was smart enough to know this should be his next move. He ordered. "Give me the best cognac in the house."

Tim was in instant denial. This can't be the mook I tossed out of here about a year ago—the one Mr. Markham was asking about. This guy's in the chips and lookin' real good. He scratched his head. Yet, ya never know. A customer calling for a refill shook Tim out of his reverie.

Blake downed his drink, paid the tab and left a $10 tip on the bar.

CHAPTER TWENTY-ONE

According to the Baron's plans, Eduardo established a set-up in San Diego, similar to that of Blake's in L.A. Large shipments began coming in via regular smuggling routes along the Southern border from Columbia and Venezuela, through Central America to Mexico and then delivered to Blake's and Eduardo's warehouses. Soon, a new ingredient was added to the mix: methamphetamine (speed).

Business was booming. The Baron was branching out, issuing instructions to be followed meticulously. He put Blake and Eduardo in touch with transportation coordinators in several states. Meetings were held and plans laid for local distribution cells where shipments would be broken down for transfer to large cities across the United States.

The tempo of vehicles—tractor trailers and trucks—increased. Warehouse lights burned late into the night. Blake became ever cautious in his transactions, as well as his personal activities. This was more than he had bargained for. He knew, one wrong move and a player is out—permanently.

It was his personal agenda that provided most of the angst. Donna was complaining about how little she saw of him.

"Why can't I come over some evenings and just hang with you? You say you're just checking on deliveries. I could help you with that. We could make it enjoyable. I'll bring sandwiches, a bottle of wine . . ."

"Donna, stop! My business is serious. I'm not there to party."

They were sitting in her apartment after grabbing a late supper locally. He had anticipated an hour or so of sexually satisfying bedtime, not this flack. Blake could feel the anger welling up in him.

Donna sensed his change of mood. "Okay, Honey. I'm sorry I bugged you."

He could tell she was as disappointed as he was in the way things were progressing. Making love had happened so infrequently, of late. He altered his mood. With his tight schedule, he couldn't afford to pass up an opportunity. Smiling, he pulled her close. "Come here, Gorgeous. I want you right now."

She melted in his arms.

*　　*　　*

On rare occasions, when Blake was neither making deals nor expecting any business activity, he would ride to Beverly Hills and pass Christine's house, hoping to get a glimpse of her. With tinted windows and the top up on his convertible, he felt safe. In fact, he had visited several restaurants thinking he might run into her. That old feeling was back. Stupidly, he was throwing caution to the wind. Still fuming about that night at the Irish Pub, he was certain he had missed seeing her there.

Taking afternoon rides alone caused him some guilt for not calling Donna and asking her to lunch. Better leave well enough alone. So far, he had the relationship fairly under control. Lately, though, she was becoming more difficult to manage. She'd begun asking questions which Blake chose not to answer. It crossed his mind that she might surprise him some night at the warehouse. That would be a bad scene for both of them.

Blake found himself constantly on the defensive, juggling his love life with his secret entrepreneurship.

One night, Donna appeared unexpectedly at his apartment. He had just returned from the warehouse. He unleashed a series of nasty and cruel remarks, reducing her to tears and protestations. "Please, Sean, I'll never do anything like this again. I'm sorry. Don't be angry. It's just that I missed you so."

In spite of his anger, he couldn't help feeling sorry for her . . . and he actually felt aroused.

Take 1. Final scene: Bedroom

*　　*　　*

In spite of her promise, Blake knew enough about women to realize that there might come another time when Donna, submitting to her emotions and desires, would cross the line again. He could only hope it wouldn't be at the warehouse. A mistake there could spell disaster. The thought gave him a queasy feeling in the pit of his stomach. The Baron tolerated no witnesses. A woman, or anyone breeching the privacy of the operation, would set in motion a series of events Blake shuddered to think about. He knew of several instances where 'outsiders' efficiently vanished and the price that had been exacted.

He muttered to himself, "Damn! I've got myself set up so well, making lots of money, making plans . . . and now I've got to worry about this broad screwing things up."

Gradually, tension got the best of him. One night, at her apartment after a late supper, he said, "Donna, you are a beautiful woman and we have fun and great sex, but . . ."

Donna didn't like where this was going and she tried to stop him. "Please, Sean, you sound like you're playing a farewell scene in a movie . . ."

"I have no choice, Darlin'. Something has developed businesswise and I'm going to be on the road most of the time, in different cities. It's not fair to keep you on the hook."

"I love you. Whatever it takes, I'm willing . . ."

He cut her off. "Donna, you'll find someone else. Forget about me—for your sake more than mine."

She was crying softly and by the time he reached the door, she emitted a wail that caused him to turn back in anger. Placing his hands firmly on her shoulders, he shook her roughly. "Stop blubbering. This is for your own good. Someday you'll understand. Even if you never do, I'm telling you this is best for both of us."

Her wailing increased. Blake reached a point where he was spiraling out of control. A hard slap to her face brought an abrupt end to her sobbing and left her whimpering, as she touched her bruised cheek. She looked at him, shock and disbelief in her eyes. "How can you treat me like this? I've always done everything you've asked of me." Her tears began tracing long, wet lines around her nose and down her cheeks. Her lips trembled.

Blake turned away, his anger subsiding. "Sorry kid. Be good to yourself." He shut the door behind him.

CHAPTER TWENTY-TWO

After DESIRE, Christine was busy reading screenplays submitted by her agent, Jack Murdock. She and Charles studied them carefully and consulted with him. His advice was always right on the dime. Their choice rested with a script called TROPICAL MADNESS, a murder mystery. The rights to the story had been bought up by Warner Bros.

"Charlie, it will seem strange to be working at a different studio, without Mr. V." She had managed to get her stipulation that Charles would be the cinematographer but she couldn't accomplish the same for Mr. V. Warner's already had contracted for a director, one who was famous for working on mystery dramas filmed in exotic places.

Casting began a month before Christine's and Charles' scheduled nuptials. Soon, a stellar cast fell into place. The romantic male lead would be played by Jackson Hughes; the villain, by Doug Michaels; and, a woman of dubious character, by Christine O'Hara.

Playing this kind of a role was a departure from Christine's previous characterizations. "I'm really so excited about this," she told Charles. Then she giggled. "But, I'm such a good girl—how will I ever convince the audience there's more than meets the eye . . ."

"All they'd have to do is interview me." He winked at her and chuckled. "Besides, you're a darned good actor. No problem.

She flashed a smile. In a serious mode, she said, "Charlie, I can hardly wait. There's so much to look forward to . . . our wedding at Mr. V.'s . . . filming on location . . ."

Charles hugged her. "You are adorable, like a little girl whose Daddy has just given her a puppy."

"Charlie, this is even better than that. I get to marry the love of my life and make a movie on an exotic island. It'll be like a honeymoon for us."

He indulged her enthusiasm but couldn't resist a cautionary remark. "Chris, these so called exotic place are not always what the commercials lead you to believe."

She pouted playfully. "You're not going to be a spoil sport, are you? I won't let you. It'll be hard work, I know, but we can still have fun, too."

Charles took her into his arms, hugged her tightly and then lifted her up, cradling her close to him. "If it's fun you're looking for, young lady, you've come to the right place."

He carried her to the bedroom where he laid her down gently on the bed. Slowly, he began to undress her, caressing her. She moaned with delight as his hands touched every sensitive part of her body.

As always, he whispered, "'Tis a consummation devoutly to be wished."

She murmured softly, "Amen."

*   *   *

Weeks passed quickly as the wedding day approached. National media made the most of the upcoming event. Hollywood was atwitter. Mr. V.'s house was a beehive of activity. Rows of chairs stood in readiness to be set up on the beach. The bride and groom would walk down a center aisle to a small, framed stage draped with flowing, soft colored chiffon panels and surrounded by an array of breathtakingly beautiful flowers, carefully arranged in huge crystal vases.

"Oh, Charlie, it's going to be like a Technicolor dream sequence."

"Yes, Darling, as long as Mother Nature plays her role well and cooperates."

"Don't even think otherwise. The muses will smile down upon us, I'm sure."

"Not to worry, we have alternate plans should the weather pose a problem. Mr. V. is prepared to move us indoors to his enclosed wrap around patio. Anyway, whatever happens, Love, at the end of the day, you will be **Mrs. Charles Markham**."

*   *   *

Many weeks had passed since Blake ended his relationship with Donna. He missed her but he couldn't take the chance of her spoiling things, especially after that last episode at her apartment. Their relationship had become too risky for him.

Business at the warehouse was booming. Every move was cautiously planned and orchestrated. No more gang bangers hovering about. Blake made it his business to meet with them early in the morning or afternoon because big deliveries and pick-ups occurred during late night hours. The only annoying occurrences were occasionally caused by the two gang leaders of the Crypts: Playboy and Animal. They referred to themselves as the C.E.O.'s of their gang and were obsessed with their own image as wheelers and dealers. Playboy, especially, looked the part he was playing out: Well-dressed, a carat diamond in each earlobe, and, was surprisingly well-spoken.

Blake, however, found him to be too curious, too much in his face. Most of the time he didn't pay attention to him until, one day, when Playboy commented, "Do much on the chick scene? Good looking guy like you . . . you're like married to this place . . ."

Blake snapped. "Don't worry your little head about me."

"I did notice a great lookin' babe here some time ago. I'd like dibs on that . . ."

"Shut the hell up!" Blake scowled, thinking, this little bastard is getting on my nerves. "You here to deal, or what?"

"Okay, okay. Don't get your ass in an uproar. Just making conversation." Playboy laughed. "If you ever need any help in the love department, just call on the Playboy."

Blake decided not to dignify the remark with an answer. Conceited turd!

With deliveries increasing and routing of drugs to local distribution cells, Blake hadn't thought much about any woman. Unusual for him—but absolutely necessary. The Baron demanded strict adherence to procedure and that left little time for romance. However, the Baron had assured Blake that once these distribution cells were efficiently operational, shipments would flow smoothly and systematically. The process would become less demanding. Blake hoped so. He was making huge bucks but his life was not his own.

*   *   *

Blake hadn't paid much attention to the newspapers, of late . . . same old, same old, he figured. Now, however, news print was full of the upcoming marriage of Christine and Charles. One night, while Blake was watching the late, late news, the reporter was gushing over the wedding plans of Christine and Charles. His reportage brought Blake's frustration full circle. He jumped up from his chair and stomped around the room, shouting, "He can't have her! I won't let him! She belongs with me, dammit!" Blake had always refused to believe that the relationship would last. In the back of his mind were other plans for Christine. "Now what?" he asked the empty room.

Besides the twitter about the wedding, TV talk shows were replete with items and commentary about Christine's anticipated new film, TROPICAL MADNESS. The principals were in place and further casting was in progress on the Warner lot. Blake was well-aware of the drill. Readings, possible screen tests . . . often the stars sat in on the procedure. That meant that Christine would be at Warner's . . . and wherever she went, so did Charles. He pondered a moment. What was it that idiot Playboy had said? . . . just call on Playboy . . ." Blake slapped his thigh. "Yes, that's it! I'll make those creeps an offer they can't refuse."

Playboy and Animal were due at the warehouse early in the a.m. to score a significant amount of product to handle the increased demand for 'meth' as well as cocaine. Methamphetamine was now readily available from Blake. The Crypts had become the dominant resource on the street—notwithstanding assassinations of the competition.

Blake tossed and turned restlessly in bed. Finally, he got up, headed for the bottles of booze which stood like sentinels on the bar and poured himself several shots of scotch. Words floated back to him. " . . . need any help in the love department, just call the Playboy."

A look of pure malice slowly crossed his face. It was four o'clock in the morning but Blake was wide awake, finalizing a plan. He had no doubts that Playboy and Animal would be perfect foils in the execution of it. Those potheads won't be able to resist the deal, he assured himself.

Blake was now on a mission.

CHAPTER TWENTY-THREE

B oth sets of parents arrived late evening, as planned, several days before the wedding. They had suggested making reservations at a local hotel, but Christine would not hear of it. "We have so much room at our house. I won't have you staying anywhere but with us." And so it was.

The next day, Charles took them all to Studio City . . . a high class, small district in the San Fernando Valley, only a few miles from L.A. After a tour of the area, they dined at Vitelli's Italian Restaurant. Christine's Mother commented: "What a lovely area. It's so different from the metropolis surrounding it."

"Like Jolson used to say, 'you ain't seen nuthin' yet'," Charles replied. "Tomorrow, we're going to Paramount which is the only studio still operating in Hollywood proper, and where Christine's first two films were made."

This news was greeted with enthusiasm. Charles continued, "At Paramount, it's strictly a guided walking tour set up with all the interesting effects tourists enjoy. They don't allow visitors on any of the sound stages but we'll pull rank."

Charles' Mom exclaimed, "Oh, what fun that will be!"

The others reacted in similar fashion.

They finished their dinner at Vitelli's and as they drove back, Charles rambled on, providing movie trivia about Paramount. "The first Cecil B. deMille and Jesse Lasky movie was filmed in an old barn near Sunset and Vine. Everything's gotten larger and grander since those days."

Christine thought to herself that she had never seen him so talkative. Charles was in charge and she loved it.

*   *   *

After their tour of Paramount, they drove downtown to see the Walk of Fame where the names of stars and celebrities are engraved in the concrete sidewalks. At this point, they were growing weary so Christine suggested they end their sightseeing and stop somewhere for dinner. There were no objections.

Charles drove them to Izzy's Deli, "the deli to the stars", he told them. 'If you look around, you may see some familiar faces." He winked at Christine. The parents were immediately on the alert.

The next morning, after a leisurely breakfast, they left for yet another tour de force, this time to Warner Bros. in Burbank. Christine told them, "It's where my next movie will be filmed, except for the island scenes . . . for those, we'll go on location. I'm really excited about that."

Charles spoke about Warner's. "The tour there will show you the inside of a real working studio—no special effects, just for show. I'll arrange for a tram to take us around to the back lots. There you'll see the facades and building fronts used in street scenes, and in some places, a practical set which has rooms inside. It'll be interesting, to say the least. You'll see how movie magic is made."

As they drove around the Warner lots, Charles provided a running commentary on the history of the movie giant and some of its stars. For their parents, as they listened, life in Hollywood was a quantum leap from the mundane to the mind-boggling. They loved every minute of it.

"Just think," Charles' Mom exclaimed, "we've seen all these wonderful places . . . but, the best is yet to come: the marriage of our wonderful children, at the home of a famous director, on a beautiful beach in Malibu! Could anything be more perfect?"

*   *   *

Blake had just returned from a quick two day visit with the Baron. He delivered records together with a large sum of cash. These transactions always required exact details regarding street sales and product distributed to transportation coordinators.

The Baron had expressed his approval of Blake's performance. "Well done, as usual, my boy. You know, you have grown invaluable to me. It is not always easy to find someone to trust and believe in . . . especially in this business."

"Yes, I know. Thank you for your confidence in me." Blake found his mind drifting to other thoughts and was taken by surprise when the Baron said, "Now, Blake, we are moving to the next level—heroin. What do you think, eh?"

Blake knew the Baron's question was rhetorical, so he just nodded his approval.

"Now, it is time for some fine scotch and Cuban cigars while we discuss this. You will be surprised at the prices and the profits to be made. You know, Blake," the Baron lowered his eyelids and said, almost in a whisper, "heroin is like being kissed by God. It is a difficult moment to retrieve, so you must never chase it . . . always let the heroin do its magic." His eyes widened and he became pensive.

Blake waited a moment then he said, "I've never tried heroin but from your description, it must be a great experience." Again, his thoughts strayed. The Baron was saying something that ended with what sounded like a warning.

" . . . and you will do well to take heed."

He didn't have a clue, but Blake said, quickly, "Yes, of course. You can depend on me."

"Good. Let's have another drink." Glasses clinked. "Remember, my boy," the Baron cautioned, "Bring no new faces or trouble to my door."

Blake remained poker-faced. So that's what he meant about taking heed.

At that moment, the Baron was wondering if he was placing too much responsibility on Blake's shoulders. Had he overestimated him?

*   *   *

The wedding day arrived, bright and sunny, and Mr. V.'s beach house was the focal point of attention. The paparazzi were asked to abstain from hounding the wedding party and were promised interviews and pix later on. In order to assure their privacy, Mr. V. procured the services of the L.A.P.D. They were more than willing to assist. The last thing anybody wanted was a three-ring circus.

Mother nature was at her finest behavior: blue skies filled with white puffs, hung over a glistening ocean, sending warm but comfortable breezes.

When Christine walked down the aisle (artificial grass covered the sand) accompanied by her father, a hush fell over all. She was breathtakingly beautiful in a draped, cream colored, ankle length satin gown. A simple crown of pearls and lace adorned her long, auburn hair and cascaded to her waist. Her jewelry consisted of a pearl lariat and pearl stud earrings. She carried a lovely bouquet in her hands.

Charles and his dad stood waiting at the foot of the aisle, each looking splendid in their finely tailored tuxedos. Christine's parents and Charles' Mom, in equally appropriate garb, took their places. Both Mothers served as Matrons of Honor; Mr. V. and Jim Green, as Best Men.

After the ceremony, on the patio, the guests and newlyweds enjoyed a gourmet array of foods; champagne flowed; a trio in the far corner, played popular tunes of the day as a vocalist belted out the lyrics, Sinatra style.

Everyone was in a wonderful mood.

Not so, the distraught figure crouched behind the wheel of his convertible. Blake's car sat in the driveway of a house with a "Rent or for Sale" sign out front. He figured, if asked, he could always say he was a realtor checking out the premises. Thoughts of seeing Christine filled his mind but vanished when a policeman approached the car. Blake quickly put the car in reverse and tore off in the opposite direction. The cop watched and shook his head. "Weirdo's." He shrugged his shoulders and returned to his post.

Blake drove, in a rage. He always thought of himself as the master of control. Not so, he realized. "But, not for long," he vowed. "I've spent my whole life fighting the odds. This is just another battle, but one I'll win, at any cost."

Obsession is the hand-maiden of revenge and Blake was its vessel.

*   *   *

Back at Mr. V.'s all was right with the world. Joy and happiness abounded.

CHAPTER TWENTY-FOUR

T he day after the wedding, Charles and Christine prepared for a brief honeymoon before filming was to begin on her new project. They arranged for a limo to take their parents to the airport that evening. Charles and Christine would drive to the little town in Mexico where they had enjoyed so much in the past. She bubbled with excitement; Charles, as usual, remained contained.

He piled their luggage into the trunk of the car and went back into the house. Christine was about to change into her traveling clothes, as she called them: a knit top over black, fitted jeans. Charles whirled her around. "Come here, young lady. Before you get all 'gussied up'—one for the road." She stifled a laugh at his archaic reference, as he lifted her tenderly, emotion clouding his eyes as they met hers.

* * *

Blissfully happy and rejuvenated after their Mexican hiatus, they headed back to L.A. At the house, Charles brought their suitcases into the bedroom and, turning to Christine, he said, "Don't bother unpacking now. I have something to show you. Wash up, put on something sexy and off we go."

"Go? Go where? Can't it wait until tomorrow. We haven't even had dinner yet . . ."

"Don't be a killjoy. Just do as I ask . . . please."

"Oh, all right, but this had better be worth it. I'm hungry . . ."

Charles laughed. "Darling, I guarantee your appetite will be sated. Everything in due time." He hugged her and kissed her on the forehead. "Now for a quick shower and change and away we go."

As they drove through Beverly Hills in the direction of Sunset Boulevard, Charles quickly made a turn onto Benedict Canyon Drive. He halted in front of an impressive pair of wrought iron gates which opened suddenly as he punched in a code at the entrance. As they drove up the driveway, framed by beautifully manicured foliage and lush, green lawns, Christine's curiosity couldn't be stifled.

"Where are we, Charlie? Whose house is this? Look at that lovely chateau! Are we invited to some special event you haven't told me about?"

"Whoa, young lady! Too many questions. Just hang in there. You'll have all the answers in a minute."

Charles pulled the car up on the circular driveway to the entrance to the house and turned off the ignition. Christine noticed there were many other parked cars around. She was bursting with curiosity.

As they entered the front door, soft music was heard above hushed voices. These voices soon burst into exclamations of "Congratulations!" Christine froze in her tracks. "Charlie, what's happening?"

"My beloved wife, this house is my wedding gift to you. This is our new home and all our friends are here to wish us well."

"But, but . . ." Her eyes widened with surprise then welled up with tears.

"How . . . when . . ." Her voice trailed off.

"I'll explain everything later. Right now, enjoy your guests and **please**," he teased, "eat something."

Many of the top luminaries of the movie industry were there. As she walked along, nibbling from the scrumptious buffet, Christine greeted friends and fellow artists.

"Oh, Charlie, I don't think there's another woman in the world as lucky as I am. I don't know how and when you arranged all this . . ." She took a deep breath. "I love you, Charles Markham."

"Not half as much as I, you." He paused. "Okay. Now that your appetite has been whetted, I believe a tour of your new domicile is in order, Mistress Markham."

*   *   *

Their realtor had promised to keep the wraps on their move, but in Hollywood there is nothing sacred. Soon, there was a frenzy of media people stalking the popular couple. In this town, it's an everyday occurrence. Thankfully, it ran its course and the newlyweds settled into their routine. As usual, the tourists on Celebrity Tours buses, which rode through neighborhoods of the rich and famous, were able to get a bird's eye view of the Markhams' home.

Blake became such a tourist after he inadvertently overheard a conversation in one of his old haunts, as he sipped a Margarita one night. He felt restless and was on his own.

1st Voice: Yeah, how about Christine O'Hara's husband buying the old Mayfair place. Heard it was a wedding present for her."

2nd Voice: She's one lucky broad—not that she doesn't deserve it. They say she's one of the most admired actors in the business.

1st Voice: Sure is.

Blake strained to hear more but the two fell silent until 1st voice asked for the tab and they left. He was now consumed with learning where the residence was, thus he became one of the gawking tourists. Seeing their palatial Mayfair only added fuel to the fire.

*   *   *

Activities at the warehouse were becoming more and more routine, as Blake established and assigned transactions to Manuel, Tony and Alfredo. They had been there from the beginning—cooperative and trustworthy. Even though Blake knew they were the Baron's moles, he had complete faith that they were there to protect him. It was essential that no attention be drawn to the warehouse. So far; so good. Blake was comfortable in his niche as the 'drug czar' to the neighborhood gangs. He was also rapidly becoming one of the important kingpins in the distribution of narcotics to major cities. The addition of heroin to his 'menu' put him well over the top financially.

However, as comfortable as he was, he was as ignorant of the surveillance by the D.E.A. The office had received a tip that something was going on at a warehouse on Central and 6th Streets. The D.E.A. was biding its time. They needed names. Until they could identify the major players, they would not show their hand. So far, they had been unable to tie any drug activity to that location. A few 'friendly' visits found stacks of TV parts and an office in pristine order, records and all. Blake played it cool, cool enough, so far, to escape any trouble.

All the officers could do was bide their time.

*   *   *

Playboy and Animal arrived at the warehouse early on the morning that Blake had devised a proposition he was certain the boys couldn't refuse.

"I want you to kill someone for me."

The remark startled the boys, at first, but not too much. They were no strangers to murder.

"What did you have in mind?" Playboy asked.

"I want you to kill Charles Markham, the husband of Christine O'Hara."

"What the hell?" Playboy snapped. "You want us to kill this guy? I dunno . . ."

"What the hell?" Blake mimicked. "Like you haven't killed anyone? This is your chance to move into the big time."

"Why do you want this guy dead?" Animal butted in.

Blake sneered. "Because the bastard stole my girl."

"**Your** girl? He's married to that gorgeous chick in the movies . . ."

"Yeah. That's right. She was mine until he turned her head."

Playboy and Animal exchanged glances. Then Playboy said, "I dunno about this. A punk on the street is one thing—but a celeb . . . I dunno."

"Come on, Playboy. You told me you're the man in the love department. Well, I need you to prove it . . . and the sooner, the better."

"I said love, not murder." Playboy hesitated. "I'll talk it over with Animal and we'll come back with an answer tomorrow morning."

"Take care of this matter and you will receive a kilo of cocaine, plus $20,000."

The boys hesitated a moment, glanced back at Blake but said nothing. They left.

After a day of doing business on the street, the two boys spoke long into the night. All that cocaine and money! Playboy considered it a hit that would enable them to live the good life on some exotic island . . . beautiful girls . . .

Animal was not as positive. "We got a great set up here. Why spoil it? And, murdering that Markham guy . . . there'll be a big brouhaha. It's not like knocking off some crack head on the street that no one cares about."

Playboy was deep in thought. "Hmm, you got a point there, but when'll we ever get our hands on a kilo of cocaine and $20,000 all at one time? I say we go for it."

Animal hesitated. "What if we get caught? We don't even know the game plan. Let's hear that before we decide."

"You got a point there. Okay. Tomorrow a.m. we check it out."

Animal could not help wondering why a chick like Christine O'Hara would have anything to do with a creep like Sean Ferguson.

*   *   *

Blake had done his homework. After several trips to Benedict Canyon Drive in his convertible, he became familiar with the layout of the grounds surrounding Christine's new home. He also spent some time on the Warners' lot to get an edge on the filming schedule for TROPICAL MADNESS. He made small talk with some of the guards. They confided that depending on how many takes and re-takes were scheduled, shooting usually stopped by dinner time.

Time was of the essence in Blake's plan. This would be tricky. His plan would only work if Christine and Charles went straight home from the studio. It was usually dark by then. He couldn't afford to have the boys parked in a private area like that for too long, with the motor running. It was sure to attract attention.

When Playboy and Animal showed up, Blake said, "Let's go for a ride."

They looked at him questioningly.

He laughed. "Come on, guys, you've got nothing to worry about. I'm going to show you how simple it will be. Piece of cake." He ushered them out to his Mercedes.

"But, we haven't exactly said Yes to anything yet," Playboy said.

Blake knew they were hooked. The offer was irresistible. "Trust me. This is an offer you can't refuse." He headed crosstown to Sunset, turning north at Will Rogers Memorial Park to Beverly Hills, and then onto Benedict Canyon Drive. As they drove by the plush and lush mansions in the area, Playboy emitted a low whistle; Animal, a "Wow!"

Suddenly, Blake cautioned, "Heads up. Pay close attention. This is where they live." He drove by slowly, stopping briefly, instructing the boys, "Observe the long driveway, the wrought iron gates, and the low brick wall which runs parallel to the property. Look at the circular driveway and the house itself." He pointed to a landscaped section abundant with foliage and bushes, flanked by several huge trees just to the left of the long driveway. "One of you will hide there. Plenty of cover. When you see their car approaching the gates, run like hell alongside the brick wall towards the house; jump the wall as they are parking in front of their door. It'll be an easy shot. Get back to the car a.s.a.p. The L.A.P.D. is known for their quick response in that area. Whichever one of you sits in the car, make sure you keep the motor running and the lights off. You'll be in a rental car, of course.

"Now I'll show you where to park." He pointed to a house that had a a For Sale sign in front, a short way down the street.

"When are we supposed to be doing this?" Playboy asked.

"As soon as possible. However, it may be more than a one shot deal." Blake grinned.

The boys did not find humor in the innuendo.

"Anyway, I expect you to go back, as necessary, until you hit the right night. If you can't catch them coming home within a reasonable time, like one-half hour, don't hang around. It'll look suspicious."

Blake drove around the block one more time. "Have a good look. Remember everything I told you, especially, that timing is everything."

They returned to the warehouse where they reviewed all the details again. At one point, Animal asked, "What about the goodies and the money?"

"All in due time, punk." Blake was annoyed by the question.

The word 'punk' did not sit well with the boys. They exchanged glances but said nothing. They took the fake I.D. he gave them and enough cash to "rent a car out of the area immediately."

When they left, Blake sat back in his chair and smiled. It always pays to plan ahead.

CHAPTER TWENTY-FIVE

TROPICAL MADNESS was right on schedule. Both the director and the producers were happy with the dailies. They would be ready for location shots within a week or so.

Christine and Charles enjoyed normal evenings at home, whenever possible.

"Charlie, I love our new place so much. I can hardly wait to get back when we finish shooting at the studio."

"I know, Sweetheart, because you never even want to stop for dinner."

"Charlie, it's such a pleasure to eat in our luxurious kitchen. I enjoy preparing meals for us."

"Or, ordering in," he teased.

"For sure!"

* * *

After their surveillance with Blake, the boys made their move the next night. At approximately seven p.m., a car slid into place in front of a house for sale on Benedict Canyon Drive. Only a fashionable lamp post flickered softly nearby in the dark. A figure in black, wearing a ninja mask, jumped out of the car and quickly disappeared. Animal sat nervously talking to himself. "Keep the motor running, lights off, be ready to take off in seconds when Playboy comes running . . ."

Suddenly, a voice interrupted, "Can I help you? What's going on?"

The sound of a gunshot penetrated the quiet night. Within seconds, Playboy came dashing out of the darkness. As the man turned toward him, Playboy jumped into the car and they sped off.

"What the hell . . . ?" The man, a neighbor, had promised to keep tabs on the house. "Good thing I took down the license plate number." He shook his head. "Never know."

He thought now about hearing what he thought sounded like a gun shot.

Within minutes, there were police cars and medical response vehicles swarming the area. The man hastened toward them. When he was told that someone had been shot, he immediately told the police about the suspicious car, its strange occupants, and the license plate number.

"Thanks," the officer in charge said. "This might be the break we need."

An ambulance took Charles to the hospital. He had been shot in the head. Christine was inconsolable and insisted upon riding with them. She was questioned briefly by the police. Because she was so distraught, she deferred answering any further questions until she was sure Charles had received all the necessary attention.

*   *   *

In the fleeing car, Playboy was rapidly shedding his black coveralls and face mask. "When we get to Sunset, pull up to a garbage disposal so we can dump these things."

Animal was a nervous wreck. "Tha-that man . . . he saw us . . ."

"Knock it off! He could never ID us. Stop being such a wuss."

Animal changed his tune. "I heard a shot, so that means we're on the money, right?"

Playboy never could resist the opportunity for self-praise. "You should have seen it," he bragged. "As the car approached the gates, I ran along the brick wall and jumped it just as they were parking in front of the house. Clipped him right in the head. His wife was hysterical—called 911 right away. She sure is a beauty."

"Wow!" Animal was in awe. "I can't believe it happened so easy."

"Easy? Waddya mean easy? I had to leap like a gazelle so the timing was right." Playboy tapped the side of his head with his forefinger. "And a little brain power didn't hurt, either."

"I could never have done it. I almost wet myself when that man came over to the car," Animal admitted, sheepishly.

"Always knew you were a pisser!"

They had a good laugh.

Back at the warehouse, Blake waited in anticipation. He sent Manuel and the men home early. No deliveries were expected that night. Blake was hoping that the boys would succeed on their first try. He didn't look forward to a prolonged situation. Too dangerous.

When the boys showed up, he could tell at once by their exuberance that they had been successful. They recounted the whole scene, how it had all gone down so well, but said nothing about the stranger who approached the car. Better left unsaid, they decided.

Animal, ever anxious, asked, "So when is the big payoff? We did the deed."

Blake studied their faces for a moment. "Boys, I trust your story is correct, but let's wait until we hear it confirmed on the news. Then we'll do business. The story should hit the papers and TV by morning . . . if not sooner."

"How's about we hang here until the late news . . . see what happens . . . close the deal?" Playboy was getting restless.

Meanwhile, word of the shooting was spreading rapidly. Late night breaking news released a statement: "Charles Markham, husband of actor Christine O'Hara, has been shot outside their home in Beverly Hills. More details to follow after further investigation by the L.A.P.D. and interviews with the doctors at the hospital."

Blake's ire was building as he listened. "Shot? Not killed? You're not saying much Playboy. Did you kill him or not?" Blake was pacing up and down, yelling.

"Looked dead to me. Got him square in the head. The guy dropped like a lead balloon." It hadn't entered his mind that perhaps the shot had not been fatal. Now, he thought, wouldn't that be a bitch after all I went through. He was egoistical enough to see himself the victim of a foiled plot.

Animal shuffled his feet nervously. He had bad vibes about the whole scenario. But, first things first. He asked Blake, "We're still getting what you promised us, right? I mean, we did get the guy."

Blake unleashed his frustration upon them. "You idiots! You nincompoops! You shot him but you don't know if you killed him. The police said 'shot', not 'killed'."

Animal said, "Maybe they're purposely saying that. You know, they don't always give the facts right away . . ."

Blake cut him off. "You better pray that's what is happening. Now, get out of here. Call me after the morning news—it better be good—and we'll take it from there."

"How's about showing a little good faith now—some of the stuff you promised." Playboy was getting up tight.

Still fuming, Blake lashed out again. "Good faith! You dumb bastards! Get out of here before I shoot you." A gun suddenly materialized in his hand.

Playboy decided to cool it. "We'll be in touch, Mr. Ferguson." He nodded to Animal and they headed for the side door.

Once outside, Animal had bad feelings. "I think he's gonna stiff us if that guy ain't dead. Maybe, even if he is. I got my doubts . . ."

Playboy cut in. "He's messing with the wrong dudes, if has any such ideas . . ." His voice trailed off. "Come on let's get some shut-eye."

*   *   *

There was nothing more definitive on the morning news. When the boys called the warehouse, he told them to return the rental car and come to the warehouse that afternoon.

Blake was strung out. Manuel noticed he was not acting his usual assured self. Plainly, Blake was a nervous wreck. When the boys arrived, Blake ushered them into his office and closed the door.

Manuel, Tony and Alfredo took a lunch break, at Blake's suggestion. "Why don't you fellas go out for a couple of brews and some tachos." Usually, a suggestion like that was greeted with enthusiasm. This time, however, not so. However, Blake didn't even notice. He just wanted them out of the way.

The midday news disclosed that the L.A.P.D. had information about a car parked in the vicinity and possibly involved in the shooting of Charles Markham. The license plate number had been provided by a neighbor who was curious about the car, parked with its lights off, motor running. Luckily, he was able to get the plate number before the car took off with another man, who suddenly appeared and jumped into the vehicle. "It was too dark to tell what they looked like," he told police.

Blake stared at the boys. In a harsh voice, he said, "You were made by some nosey body in the street? He got the plate number? How the hell did that happen?" He was shouting at the top of his lungs. "Somehow, you forgot to mention that."

Animal jumped in. "I swear, he came over to the car just as Playboy came running. I didn't even see the guy until he practically had his face against the window, asking if I needed help. Don't know when or how he got the plate number . . . it happened so fast . . . it was so dark. He couldn't identify anyone, if he tried."

"Yeah, stupid! How about the car rental? Think anyone there could recognize you?" Blake was furious.

"The place is miles away in Long Beach. We used the fake ID you gave us. We returned it early this morning. Place wasn't even open yet . . . left the car in the parking lot."

Just then, a TV newscaster was announcing the latest development in the Markham shooting. Blake turned up the volume. " . . . and so the surveillance camera outside the car rental office captured the license plate of a car driven by one of the renters of the car suspected of being involved in last night's shooting. A 'bolo' has been issued by the police: "*Be on the lookout* for this car and report any sightings of it to the police."

The three sat stunned for a moment. Blake exploded. "You assholes! You parked your vehicle in plain sight? Did you lame brains ever hear about security cameras?"

Playboy and Animal began speaking at the same time, stumbling over each other's words. Blake shut them up with a warning: "You'd better keep quiet about this. Get out of town—disappear. Get rid of your car and the gun."

What a damn mess he'd gotten himself into. Blake was running scared now. If the Baron gets wind of this . . . don't even go there. These punks better keep their mouths shut—and Charles better be dead.

When the men returned from their long lunch, they could hear the raised voices from behind the closed office door. They couldn't see the package in Blake's hand which contained the $20,000 he had hastily wrapped and handed to Playboy, saying, "When this matter is settled, you'll receive the balance of our agreement. Remember, if the subject is not a **dead** issue, you'll get nothing more."

Playboy and Animal were not too happy about it, however, they had no options.

"We'll be in touch," Playboy said.

"Remember, just keep your mouths shut," Blake warned, "if you want to enjoy the fruits of your labor."

Playboy's temper was surfacing. He didn't take crap like this from anyone. Pursing his lips, he spat out the words. "If anyone should be worried about that, I think you are the most likely candidate."

Blake cooled it. These crazies were not to be messed with. "Okay, boys, be in touch. Meanwhile," he repeated, "get rid of your car and the gun."

When the boys exited the office, they passed Manuel as they headed for the side exit. "*Adios, amigo,*" Playboy said.

"*Adios.*" Manuel nodded as he locked the door behind them. He was not oblivious to the package Playboy carried and he wondered what had transpired behind that closed office door. All that shouting—it sounded like trouble. He had always been privy to every transaction. This puzzled him.

He spoke with Tony and Alfredo. "I think I should mention this to the Baron."

The men agreed.

CHAPTER TWENTY-SIX

Throughout the night, Christine sat at Charles' hospital bed, tears streaming down her face as she held his hand in hers. His head was bandaged and he was barely lucid. The connection to various monitoring devices indicated the seriousness of his condition.

"Oh, my darling, why did this awful thing happen? Who could have wanted this?" Her voice was a hoarse whisper; her sorrow was uncontrollable.

Charles attempted to smile. He tried to squeeze her hand as best he could. Luckily, the bullet had missed the brain and lodged itself in the side of his skull. Quick action by the medics and surgeon at the hospital prevented extensive damage. It would take some time. The surgeon told Christine, "The prognosis is good. He needs time to rest and recuperate."

"I'll see to that, you can be sure." She thanked him for all he had done.

The motive for the shooting was a puzzle. It was obvious that robbery was not but that Charles, himself, had been the mark. L.A.P.D. probed all the possibilities. Did Charles have a disagreement with anyone on the set at the studio? Trouble with a neighbor? Even, trouble with a lover? Every avenue was exhausted but the police came up with nothing.

A check on the license plate of the car of interest resulted in some information. The car had been rented from Drive Safely Car Rentals in Long Beach. The clerk there told them the renter was a Paul Smith whose driver's license indicated he lived in Long Beach. This proved to be a dead end. Shortly thereafter, the police were alerted to another car and its license plate number captured by the surveillance cameras in the parking lot of the Drive Safely Car Rentals. This time, the computer brought up the name of an Anthony Bardo, residing at 1389 Pico Blvd., Los Angeles.

Detectives Murphy and Shapiro were immediately dispatched to that address. They ascertained the apartment number from a mailbox in the front entrance of the building. There was no answer to their knock on the door. As they stood there, an elderly lady approached them, saying, "They're hard to find at home. The boys keep crazy hours. I always wonder about that. Anyway, they never bother anybody. Are they in trouble?"

"No, nothing's wrong. We just wanted to ask them a few questions, that's all," they told her. "Thanks for your help."

They returned to their car where they sat awhile, further down the street, making notations for their report. Looking in the rear view mirror, they saw a car pull up to the building they had just left. Two boys jumped out of the car, leaving the motor running, and ran into the house. The detectives quickly turned their vehicle around and as they approached, the boys came dashing out, threw some baggage in the trunk and quickly sped away. The detectives, in pursuit, called for back up as they approached a large intersection. The boys were in the car in front of them. Traffic had come to a standstill. L.A.P.D. vehicles were approaching in all directions and motorists were pulling over to the side to let them through.

Playboy and Animal were trapped.

"What'll we do?" Animal was panicking.

"Just be cool. You don't know anything. Remember, we were high on drugs and don't remember a thing." Playboy's demeanor did not betray the turmoil in his own mind.

"Get out and put your hands on the back of your head," Murphy ordered.

Shapiro walked around to the back of the car and checked the plates. "This is the car all right." He looked closely at the boys, studying them for a moment. "Hey, I know these kids. They were questioned last year on suspicion of dealing on the street. Remember?"

"Right," Murphy answered. "Let's get the drug sniff dog here. Maybe we'll get lucky. We can hold them on that."

Shapiro called in the request. The dog keyed the car immediately. This gave the detectives probable cause to search the car but, because the vehicle was suspected of being used in an attempted homicide, the detectives had the car impounded for a thorough search.

The boys were handcuffed, Mirandized and taken to Parker Center where they were ushered into separate interrogation rooms. L.A.P.D.

believed they had two viable suspects in the attack on Charles Markham. All they needed now was to prove it.

For the rest of their lives, Playboy and Animal would regret not having followed Mr. Ferguson's advice to get rid of their car and the gun.

*   *   *

As Blake was preparing for a late night delivery, as usual, he kept the TV on. He heard a reporter announce the arrest of two suspects, Anthony Bardo and Timothy Simmons, who were presently being held for possession of an illegal substance; that it is believed that the car they were driving is somehow related to the attempted homicide of Charles Markham, husband of Christine O'Hara.

At the time of this announcement, Blake was eating in. Manuel had brought him a quesadilla and a large, black coffee. When Blake heard the news of the arrest, he jumped up from his chair, overturning his coffee, shouting, "Merde! Those stupid little shits!" He didn't need anyone to tell him who Anthony Bardo and Timothy Simmons were.

Working in the bay, the men stopped what they were doing and looked up in surprise. Manuel ran into the office, asking, "What's wrong? We heard your shouts . . ."

Blake composed himself. "Nothing. Everything's all right. I just made a bad bet . . . cost me some money, that's all." He changed the subject, asking, "Everything ready for the delivery?"

"Yes. This will be one of the biggest deals we have made. The Baron is most anxious about it."

"There should be no problem." Blake tried to be casual. "Just let them do the usual check of the product and you check the money. They're reliable people."

When the deal was completed and a million and-a-half dollars was added to the hiding place in the wall, the men left for the night. Now alone, Blake ran his fingers through his hair and then held his head tightly with both hands. He felt like it was ready to explode.

"God, what have I gotten myself into? Damn you, Christine!" Within a moment, fear filled his being. What if the Baron gets wind of my involvement in the shooting? He had to make sure that never happens. But how? Lately, he has been acting strangely, he had to admit. Did Manuel and the men suspect any improprieties? Equally as important—will those two punks incriminate him?

CHAPTER TWENTY-SEVEN

I n desperation, Blake did something he thought he'd never do again. He called Donna Golden. If things get really sticky, he would need a safe house. Blake wondered who would get to him first, the L.A.P.D. or the Baron? Or, he optimistically considered, perhaps by some lucky fluke, he would escape any involvement. Reality had soon set in, hence the decision to seek out a haven.

When she answered the phone, he said nothing more than that he missed her and wanted to see her.

Donna welcomed him with open arms. "I prayed you'd come back to me. I missed you so."

"I missed you too, Baby." Typical Blake. He kissed her passionately.

They heard the news over breakfast. "Two youths originally held for possession of illegal drugs are new being questioned in the attempted homicide of Charles Markham. A gun, found in the glove compartment of their impounded car, is being checked for fingerprints. It is believed to be the weapon used in the assault upon Mr. Markham."

Blake was fuming. He was careful not to let his true feelings show.

Donna was saying, " . . . and I feel sorry for kids like that, getting high on drugs and doing things they don't even remember doing."

"Yeah. You know, I think those kids are from the neighborhood Downtown. They ran errands for me a couple of times . . . never took them for druggies. Wish I could help . . ."

"What could you do?" Donna looked at her hero with admiration in her eyes.

"Maybe get them a good lawyer. I wish I could tell them that, but as a businessman in the area, I can't really get involved."

Sweet, gentle, misguided Donna asked, "Could I help? Tell me."

"That's so great of you, but I wouldn't think of getting you involved . . ."

She cut him off. "Just tell me. I'd do anything for you."

Before Blake could answer, another breaking news announcement blared on the TV. "The two youths, now viable suspects, are being charged with felony assault in the Charles Markham shooting. They have requested a lawyer. Thus far, they have said nothing more than to insist they were high on drugs that night and do not remember anything. Their fingerprints, processed through IAFIS, revealed they had a history of a prior arrest for possession of an illegal substance for which they served time in a juvenile facility."

Blake was now caught in a web. He knew that with their backs to the wall, their attorney would look for a loophole to cop a plea—and he was that loophole.

Donna was aware of Blake's agitation. He just sat there, mind racing, saying nothing. "Honey, what is it?"

"It's nothing, Donna. Forget about it." He paused. "Listen, I've got to get back to the warehouse. Got some business to take care of. Call you later." He kissed her quickly on the cheek and hastened out the door before she could object.

Donna just stood there, speechless. Whatever that business was, somehow she knew something was terribly wrong. That old, bad feeling was back.

*   *   *

Blake was anxious to return to the warehouse because he knew his absence would raise more questions. He also realized that he had to make a move. A big one.

Manuel told him that detectives had been there asking questions. "They showed us pictures of that Playboy and Animal. The police say they were investigating a shooting. We said nothing to them. What is happening, Blake?"

"Not to worry. The boys must have gotten into a little trouble, that's all."

The men couldn't help but notice that Blake's demeanor did not match is words. He looked like a frightened animal.

The next morning, Manuel left for Mexico. The Baron had requested the latest accounting of transactions, together with a substantial portion of the cash on hand. It was not unusual for Manuel to make such trips. It freed up more time for Blake to handle things at the warehouse. Blake usually welcomed this advantage, however, when Manuel left this time, he had an uneasy feeling. However, he told him, "Have a good trip and my best regards to the Baron."

Later, alone in his office, Blake reflected upon the Baron's warning: Bring no new faces or trouble to my door.

And he had done exactly that.

*   *   *

When the Baron and Manuel finished their business, they shared the customary scotch on the rocks and a Cuban cigar. Manuel took the opportunity to mention Blake's strange behavior.

At first, the Baron showed no concern. Instead, he spoke at length about the success of their heroin enterprise. "Remember how we had to get supplies from Columbian smugglers? Columbian white . . . good stuff, eh? Our customers loved it. No need for injections, just inhale or smoke. Now we produce our own 'black tar heroin'—*que bueno.*"

Manuel sat and said nothing. He was wondering why the Baron was reiterating things they had discussed many times before. However, he added, "Yes, I know, and as you instructed us, we warn our transporters not to distribute it in its purest form, that the strength must be cut or it can be deadly."

"The 25% pure is enough for users and, for us, the profits are even better." The Baron puffed heavily on his cigar, looking pensive. Suddenly, he said, "Manuel, I sense you have some doubts regarding Blake. I have always trusted your opinion. Pay close attention."

"*Seguramente.* I will."

*   *   *

Manuel returned to L.A. the next day. Tony and Alfredo complained to him. "Blake is acting strange. He is running in and out of here like a nervous puppy. We are lucky the shipments are moving on schedule."

"Maybe he is not feeling well," Manuel looked at them knowingly. He repeated the Baron's advice to him. "Pay close attention." His voice implied more than his words.

CHAPTER TWENTY-EIGHT

Detectives Murphy and Shapiro, acting on a court order, did a search of the boys' apartment. They found a scene in complete disarray: refuse and empty bottles everywhere, indicative of a hasty departure. With the usual propensity for checking every miniscule of possible evidence, they patiently sifted through the trash.

Murphy suddenly called to Shapiro. "This might be something." He carefully unfolded and examined a slip of paper bearing a phone number with the notation, Private Mr. F.

Shapiro immediately called the number on his cell phone. A recorded message responded: "At the beep, leave your name, order, the next day pick up time." A trace on the phone revealed it belonged to a Sean Ferguson, TV Parts and Supplies, at Central and 6th Street in L.A.

"Pay dirt!" Murphy shouted. "Isn't that the warehouse that was under surveillance from time to time?"

Shapiro agreed. "Let's get back to headquarters, pronto! The Captain's going to love this."

The Captain was on the media every day, lauding the work of his men who were "closing in on the guilty perpetrators in the Charles Markham shooting." Now he announced that another arrest was expected soon.

*　　*　　*

The District Attorney met with the lawyer representing Anthony Bardo and Timothy Simmons. "My clients are willing to cooperate in this investigation and will do so for certain concessions," the lawyer told him.

When asked what concessions the boys were looking for, he said, "They will give you the identity of the person behind the attack as well as the reason for it. This they will do in exchange for a lighter sentence, with the possibility of parole at an early date."

The D.A. offered them five years, with the possibility of parole in two. He told them that his leniency was based upon the fact that the boys were young, had only one recorded arrest in the system and, most importantly, their willingness to cooperate and divulge important information.

The offer was accepted.

Because the detectives had already obtained the name of a person of interest, the boys' information and identification was important. It might be just what was needed to bring the case to a close.

Playboy and Animal attested to the following: That Sean Ferguson was their drug supplier. That his place of business was at 628 Sixth Street, Los Angeles, and that is where they obtained their drugs. That Mr. Ferguson was obsessed with the actor, Christine O'Hara and that he, Mr. Ferguson, wanted her husband, Mr. Charles Markham, dead.

Furthermore, that Mr. Ferguson claimed that Ms. O'Hara was a former girlfriend of his. That they (the suspects) were enticed by Mr. Ferguson, with money and drugs, to kill Mr. Markham. That the night of the shooting, both boys were high on heroin, supplied by Mr. Sean Ferguson.

The media had a heyday. The public was asked to call the L.A.P.D. with any information. A special phone number was assigned for that purpose. The Captain announced, "When the guilty person is apprehended and in custody, we are sure it will bring this bizarre case to a close."

*   *   *

At the warehouse, behind the closed door to his office, Blake removed half-a-million in cash from his wall 'safe', put the money into a valise and placed it under his desk. He then called Manuel in to discuss the current transactions, which easily reflected the large amount of money stashed away next to Blake's feet. Time was of the essence.

"Manuel, you and your men are good soldiers. Thank you for handling things while I have been so busy lately. It was a family matter that needed my attention." He was banking on the fact that they had not heard the latest news.

A poker faced Manuel replied, "No problem."

Blake suggested, 'I'll be here for now. There's nothing scheduled until late tonight. Why don't the three of you enjoy a break?" He pulled out a $100 bill from his wallet. "A little tequila wouldn't be bad, eh?"

"Thank you, Blake." Manuel hastened out of the office. The men left immediately, locking the door behind them. Once they drove out of sight, Manuel placed a call to the Baron. "We have a problem. The 'animals' are sniffing around, asking questions—and asking for Mr. Sean Ferguson. I'm sure our friend is in trouble. The newspapers are full of the shooting of Mr. Charles Markham and the police are holding two boys who have done business with us . . ."

The Baron interrupted. "Be prepared to close down the operation tonight. I will advise the necessary people. Expect a call from me within the hour." He put down the phone slowly and wondered about the circumstances that brought detectives to the warehouse in the first place. The Baron dialed the special number for Blake.

When his phone rang, Blake's jagged nerves propelled him out of his chair. He recognized the number immediately. It was the Baron. He shook as he gingerly picked up the phone and answered. "Hello, Baron."

"Blake, my boy, how are you? I hear you have not been so well these past few days."

"Nothing to worry about . . . a little family problem . . . everything's fine now." Blake was in a sweat. Damn—Manuel must have said something.

"You know, my boy, you are working too hard. You need a few days here at the mansion. Some fine scotch, Cuban cigars, beautiful *senoritas*—best medicine in the world."

Blake's mind was in turmoil. He knew he couldn't refuse. "Sounds good to me. I'll drive down tonight. The ride will relax me. Thanks."

"Good," was followed by the usual click.

Blake shuddered as he recalled a warning from Iggy when he first started working on those trips to the Baron. "Don't ever try to fool them. You'll end up in a body bag. They'll blow your brains out—or decapitate you on the spot—or both."

He knew he had to make a decisive move. Grabbing his valise from under the desk, he locked the side and bay doors and jumped into his car. At the Orlando, he quickly packed a suitcase and hurried down to the lobby. As he rushed out, the desk clerk took little notice. Mr. Ferguson was always rushing in and out.

As Blake approached his car, his mind scrambled rapidly over several alternatives. Go to the Baron and confess all? No way. He remembered the warning. Take Donna and escape to places unknown . . . she would only be excess baggage. Fly to New York? "Yes, that's it! At least, I have people there. I can be Blake Dugan again," he assured himself. He smiled at the thought.

As he bent to put his luggage into the trunk of the car, he felt a hard object in his back. A voice warned him to be quiet. "You will ride with us, *Senor.*"

*   *   *

The call within the hour that the Baron had promised Manuel was brief and to the point. "I am afraid that our friend will soon be sick (arrested). It is time to put on the wedding rings and let the honeymoon begin. Send him to Heaven."

When he hung up, a sadness overwhelmed him. He had a fondness for Blake. As he puffed on his cigar, he thought, Blake was one of my best . . . foolish man to get involved with those boys and the shooting. The Baron sighed heavily. Now I had to order his execution . . . but, he has endangered the organization . . . he must pay the price.

When the Baron sat down to dine that evening, surrounded by his cadre and beautiful women, he poured brandy into a snifter and toasted his guests. He said nothing of the drama about to play out on the highway from Los Angeles to Mexico.

CHAPTER TWENTY-NINE

A confused and unhappy Donna sat transfixed as she listened to the news announcement of the identity of a Mr. Sean Ferguson, allegedly the person behind the shooting of Mr. Charles Markham. She couldn't believe what she was hearing. She shouted at the TV set, "They've made a terrible mistake!"

She thought she could help absolve him by calling police headquarters and telling them just that. Donna agreed to come down to speak with them. Once there, she explained that Sean Ferguson was in business in a warehouse which her office rented to him; that the business was a TV parts and supplies source, and, coincidentally, he was her boyfriend.

"Do you happen to know his place of residence?" the detective asked.

"Of course. He lives at the Orlando, in town."

The officers couldn't believe their luck. This may be the break they were waiting for.

"Thanks for your help. We'll be in touch."

Before she left, Donna insisted, "You will clear this up, won't you? Mr. Ferguson would never be involved in something like this."

"Yeah, sure. Thanks again."

When she left, Detectives Murphy and Shapiro were immediately dispatched to the Orlando hotel. There, the desk clerk confirmed, "Mr. Ferguson is indeed staying with us. However, he's not in. He went rushing out of here a couple of hours ago. Off on another business trip, I suppose."

"Thanks." The detectives hurried out.

Back at headquarters, they immediately manned the phones, checking airlines for a possible reservation. No results. An A.P.B. was issued for his car. Following protocol, a court order was obtained to search the warehouse.

Donna agreed to meet them there with the key to the premises. When they entered, they found an empty bay and office . . . not a single sign that a business had been conducted there. Everything was wiped clean.

Donna was on the verge of tears. What had happened here? Why would Sean leave without telling her? She was trying so hard to help clear his name. She began to sob.

Murphy and Shapiro exchanged glances. Dealing with emotional women was never easy. Detective Shapiro offered, "Would you like us to drive you home? You're upset . . . not good to drive in that state."

"No, no thanks." Donna dabbed at her eyes and blew her nose noisily into a tissue. She felt foolish. "I'm okay now. If you're done here, I'll lock up."

"We're done. Thanks for your cooperation," Detective Murphy said. "We'll be in touch."

Driving home, Donna had mixed emotions. What if the police were right? Sean did have a dark side to him. What about those boys? No, it can't be true . . . but, if it is? How could I have been so misled by him . . . so willing to tolerate his abusive behavior? Only fools fall in love like I did—blindly.

She parked her car and hastened up to her apartment, half-hoping he'd be there and hoping he wouldn't. Closing the door behind her, she rushed over to the answering machine. No call. No message.

Somehow Donna knew there would never be another call.

*   *   *

Charles Markham was making a remarkable recovery. "Thanks to my wonderful wife," he would tell visitors.

When the detectives showed him photographs of Bardo and Simmons, Charles said, apologetically, "I'm sorry. I can't help you. It all happened so quickly, I never got a look at the shooter."

Christine spent every possible minute with Charles. With a nurse to look after him, Christine was able to finish the final home scenes for TROPICAL MADNESS at the studio. The plans to go on location would be delayed by agreement with Warner Bros. until Christine was free to travel. She had insisted that would happen when Charles was well enough to travel with her. Fortunately, the filming was ahead of schedule so it was arranged.

Meanwhile, the L.A.P.D. had ordered 24/7 surveillance at their home. "Better safe than sorry," the Captain told them. "We do still have another suspect at large."

When Jim Green came to visit, they would spend time speculating about the shooting.

Christine would ask, over and over again, "Why would anyone want to do such a terrible thing? Charles is such a good person and so well liked."

Jim had his own suspicions but this wasn't the time to speculate. He wanted Charles to stay calm and recover as quickly as possible. "The world is full of kooks. There's no telling what sets off a spark with some people."

When Christine and Charles were alone, Christine sat on the edge of his bed, stroking his face and kissing him. "Darling, I don't know what I would have done if . . ."

"Shush, Chris. I'm here. I'll always be here for you."

"Mr. Markham, I do so love you to d . . . .". She quickly caught herself. "I love you madly."

He laughed at her almost-faux pas. "Right back at you!"

One evening, listening to the news, they heard about the latest developments in the case: the confessions of Anthony Bardo and Timothy Simmons. They definitely identified Mr. Sean Ferguson, a drug dealer, as the person behind the plot to kill Mr. Charles Markham, husband of Christine O'Hara. Even more shocking was their statement which gave the reason for the planned murder.

Timothy Simmons described Ferguson as "tall, dark complexioned, good looking; dark hair and wearing a mustache. He was a big supplier of drugs."

The other youth, Anthony Bardo, added, "He sure was hung up on Christine O'Hara. He said she was his girl friend before Mr. Markham stole her away."

That last comment caused Christine and Charles to look at each other with a sudden realization. "Blake!" they shouted simultaneously.

*   *   *

Late, one night, a truck pulled into a small Mexican town and drove down a deserted road to the village dump. The driver told his companions, "Throw this garbage where it belongs."

Several plastic bags, bearing their gruesome contents, were left near a huge pile of debris. The men set the bags on fire and quickly jumped back into the truck.

As they drove off, Manuel reached for his cell phone. "*Senor*, the delivery has been made."

"*Bueno*."

CHAPTER THIRTY

MEXICO, 1999

When the guard at the garbage dump in Tzurumutaro was alerted by the screams of the old lady, the police were called and an ambulance was summoned from the Coroner's Office in Mexico City.

Even though such cadavers were not an unusual occurrence, Medical Examiner Lopez wondered about the decapitated, dismembered, burnt corpse. He commented to his assistant, "Poor man, stripped, murdered, and tossed into the dustbins of history, like so many others."

"Probably another drug deal gone wrong," the assistant said.

"For sure. Look at the bruises on the wrists—what's left of them. He was handcuffed. There is a single gunshot wound to the back of the head. No doubt shot at close range and then decapitated."

The assistant nodded. "An execution body dump. The m.o. of the cartels."

M.E. Lopez continued with his examination. An assessment of the pubic bone had confirmed the corpse was a male. He approximated age by skull fusion and the victim's teeth, the shape of which told him the corpse was Caucasian. A measure of the femur bone established the height of the victim.

M.E. Lopez shook his head sadly. "All this we can determine through forensic examination . . . but who is this unfortunate soul?" He had asked this question too many times in the course of his career—too many times with no answers.

He completed his report and filed it with the proper authorities.

Get Published, Inc!
Thorofare, NJ 08086
02 February, 2010
BA2010033

suppress her tears of joy as she shamelessly embraced and kissed Charles.

As in any romantic Hollywood tale, the lovers walked hand in hand into the sunset.

Fade to black.

EPILOGUE

A small item appeared in local Mexican newspapers noting the discovery of another cadaver in the dump at Tzurumutaro. The remains of Blake Dugan, alias Sean Ferguson, were written off as an "unclaimed and unidentified John Doe."

* * *

When the trail leading to Sean Ferguson grew cold, Detectives Murphy and Shapiro of the L.A.P.D. agreed that the suspect "seems to have disappeared off the face of the earth".

* * *

On October 16th, 1999, the premiere of TROPICAL MADNESS at Grauman's Chinese was a spectacular event.

As Christine and Charles walked, hand in hand, down the red carpet, they were enthusiastically welcomed by fans lining the streets. Christine held Charles' hand, as she had done in the past, only now it was even more meaningful.

When the film ended and Christine and her co-stars stood for their accolades, she insisted that Charles stand with her. This gesture of love created a tumultuous roar of approval. Christine could not